MORE DESIRE, O1
VOLUME 1

Desire for Three: Winning Back Jesse
Blade's Desire: Adoring Kelly

Leah Brooke

MENAGE EVERLASTING

Siren Publishing, Inc.
www.SirenPublishing.com

A SIREN PUBLISHING BOOK
IMPRINT: Ménage Everlasting

MORE DESIRE, OKLAHOMA, VOLUME 1
Desire for Three: Winning Back Jesse
Blade's Desire: Adoring Kelly
Copyright © 2014 by Leah Brooke

ISBN: 978-1-62741-319-0

First Printing: May 2014

Desire for Three: Winning Back Jesse
Blade's Desire: Adoring Kelly
    Cover design by Les Byerley
Print cover design by Siren-BookStrand
All art and logo copyright © 2014 by Siren Publishing, Inc.

Printed in the U.S.A.

PUBLISHER
Siren Publishing, Inc.
www.SirenPublishing.com

SIREN
Publishing

DESIRE, OKLAHOMA

HOTEL

Ménage Everlasting

DESIRE FOR THREE:
WINNING BACK JESSE

The
Leah Brooke

Collection

DESIRE FOR THREE: WINNING BACK JESSE

Desire, Oklahoma

LEAH BROOKE
Copyright © 2014

Chapter One

Humming a tune that had been in her head all day, Jesse Erickson opened the front door, juggling her purse and the bags of food in her hands. Her body also hummed with anticipation, a sensation she wondered if she'd ever get used to. Laughing to herself, she hurried her steps, eager to find her gorgeous husbands.

She wouldn't have believed it possible to be this happy, or to feel this loved.

When she'd first arrived in Desire, Oklahoma, she'd been shocked at the lifestyles people lived here. Ménage marriages were prevalent in Desire, but after being in one bad marriage, she certainly didn't want another, especially one in which she would be married to not one, but *two* men.

Just the thought of ever tying herself to another man again had given her chills.

Yet, here she stood, two years later, anxious to get to the men who'd consumed her thoughts all day, as they did every day.

Smiling to herself at the now-familiar flood of desire that warmed her from within each time she thought about them, she started toward the kitchen, anxious for the kisses and cuddles that would be waiting for her.

And the more erotic moments that would come later.

As always, she couldn't wait.

Hearing the low rumble of her husbands' voices, she grinned and hurried her steps, stopping abruptly at the strange timbre in Clay's voice.

Although he spoke in low tones, his deep voice carried, the tenseness in it putting her on alert. "This is going to turn her world upside down. It's important that she feels loved and secure. We've got to go meet again tonight. Thank God, Jesse doesn't suspect a thing. She thinks we're going to the club."

What the hell?

Jesse paused, wondering if she'd heard him right.

Rio sighed, and Jesse could imagine his usually smiling face hard, his jaw clenching.

"I'm sure Jesse already suspects something. She's going to be crazy when she finds out. I'm tired of having to hide this from her."

What the hell could they possibly be hiding from her?

Clay cursed soundly. "What the hell are we supposed to do? She's knee-deep in work at the store, especially since Kelly's not there. We can't just blurt something like this out to her, especially now."

Her legs gave out, the deep stab of hurt more than she could bear. With her legs like rubber, Jesse dropped onto the arm of the chair where she'd sat on her husbands' laps many times.

"She's going to suspect we're hiding something from her soon."

Jesse's stomach knotted. *It couldn't be. No. Another woman?*

No, please no!

The words kept ringing in her head as her world crumbled around her.

She didn't want to believe it, but what else could it be?

She'd been expecting something like this ever since the day she'd married them, finding it difficult to believe that two men like Clay and Rio could ever be happy with someone like her.

They'd disappeared often and had the days to themselves while she ran the store.

How could she have allowed herself to become so blind? Why hadn't she suspected anything?

Although both men were closing in on fifty, they easily looked, and had the stamina of men ten years younger. Rich and gorgeous, both men stood almost six and a half feet tall and had the strength of men much younger.

She'd thought it would happen slowly. She wasn't prepared for this!

They could marry someone much younger, and have the children she could no longer bear.

Her insides turned to jelly, her mind so numb she had to struggle to think. She only knew she had to get out of here until she could gather her thoughts again, and decide what to do.

"She's going to be hurt. There's nothing we can do about that. Jesse feels things deeply, sometimes too deeply." Clay sounded even angrier than before, but she was too numb to care.

She loved them more than they were comfortable with.

"She's already been so worried about her sister, Nat, and the problems she and Jake have been having. Let's see if we can get her mind off of everything this weekend. The boys are out of town, and we'll have Jesse to ourselves. She won't even have time to think about anything else."

Jesse had indeed been looking forward to this weekend, when her son and theirs would be on the camping trip they'd been planning for weeks. Now, she wished the boys were here as a buffer between her and her husbands. Having them here would have helped her settle.

It struck her that she'd never felt that way with Clay and Rio before. Memories of her first marriage came back to her in a rush, and the emotionally draining confrontations at the end.

Suddenly, she felt tired, and older than she'd felt in a long time. She couldn't seem to find the energy to stand, but she knew she couldn't let them find her like this.

It could be nothing. It could all be some sort of terrible mistake.
It had to be.

She didn't want to believe it.

She could have misunderstood them the same way they'd misunderstood her one day long ago—a day they'd kicked her out amid angry words and harsh accusations.

She got clumsily to her feet, still gripping the bags from the diner in town. Her mouth had watered for the fried chicken she'd smelled all the way home, but now she felt like she'd throw up if she tried to eat it.

Drawing a deep breath, she tried unsuccessfully to force a smile and made her way into the kitchen, not quite ready for a confrontation.

Clay, leaning against the counter, came forward immediately, his welcoming smile so familiar and beloved she wanted to cry.

"Hey, baby. I didn't hear you come in." Frowning, he bent, brushing her hair back from her face, his eyes filled with concern. "What is it? What's wrong? Are you hurt? You're white as a sheet!"

Jesse released her hold on the bags, letting Rio take them from her. "I'm fine, just really tired." She went willingly into Clay's arms, needing his strength now more than ever.

When Rio cursed and closed in behind her, surrounding her with their strength and warmth, she found herself blinking back tears.

Rio's lips touched her hair as his strong hands ran up and down over her arms as though he could give her his strength by doing so.

In the past, it had worked, but not today.

"I knew that store was too much for you to handle. You're getting too busy and you're short-handed. Jesse, honey, I know you love the store, but I hate seeing you this way."

Clay, the older and more domineering of the two brothers she'd fallen in love with and married, lifted her against him, settling her legs around his waist.

"That's it. The store's closed. It's taking way too much of your time and energy."

Jesse pushed away from him and disentangled herself from Rio's hold. "I'm not closing the store. Look, I just want to be alone for a little while. I think I'm going to go out for a while."

She didn't want to stay at home with them tonight until she could work some things out in her head. She hated this weakness, especially after having become accustomed to feeling so strong and secure.

Marriage to Clay and Rio had changed her life, both of them showering her with more love than she'd ever thought possible. They'd blanketed her in safety and happiness and taught her to trust again.

Now, it was over, and it hurt so much, she could hardly breathe. Her stomach hurt, the feeling of emptiness making her feel hollow inside. Empty.

It had to be a mistake, but she couldn't confront them now. She wasn't ready.

Would she ever be ready?

Eyeing her thoughtfully, Rio shared a look with Clay. "We have something to do tonight, but I was going to cancel and stay home here with you."

Jesse swallowed heavily. "You didn't tell me about having plans tonight. Where are you going?"

"Just to the club."

Suddenly a lot of things made sense to her, things that she hadn't given a second thought to before. Turning away, she nodded, her neck so stiff with tension that even that small movement proved difficult. "I see."

Clay gripped her arm and yanked her around to face him. "What the hell's wrong with you?"

His anger stripped away some of the numbness, the ensuing shock of emotion slamming into her stealing her breath.

With tears blurring her vision, she slapped his hand away, bracing herself against the confusion and hurt in his eyes.

"Nothing's wrong with me except I was stupid enough to believe you. I was stupid enough to believe—never mind. Just leave me alone."

"Never."

Clay's face, hard with frustration, tightened even more. "I don't know what the hell's wrong with you, Jesse Erickson, but we're going to have this out right now."

To her horror, Jesse began to cry, deep, heaving sobs that made it impossible to talk, and nearly impossible to breathe.

The shocked look on her husbands' faces blurred, as tears filled her eyes. Holding a hand up, she shook her head, backing away. "I need a m–minute."

Turning, she ran into the bathroom and slammed the door behind her, locking it with a dead bolt they would never be able to get through.

The master bedroom had been designed as a safe room for her when her life had been in danger. It had been her haven then, but the fact that Clay and Rio had been racing to her rescue made her feel safer than any lock ever could.

Rio's insistent knock at the door made her jump. "Jesse, open this fucking door right now! Whatever's bothering you, we'll work it out together."

Jesse struggled to brace herself emotionally, and rebuild the wall that she'd used to keep her emotions safe, the wall Clay and Rio had torn down with alarming ease two years earlier.

Drawing a shaky breath, she eyed the window. "I want you to answer a question."

Clay answered, his voice low and coming from only an inch or two from the other side of the door.

"Of course, Jesse. You know you can ask us anything. We've always talked about everything, haven't we?"

Jesse had to swallow the lump in her throat before speaking again.

"Have you been keeping something from me—something to do with all the times you've gone out, telling me you were going to the club, but going to meet someone instead?"

The stunned silence coming from the other side of the door was like a knife to her heart. Not bothering to wait around for whatever excuse they would come up with, one she knew they would make her believe, Jesse unlocked the window and made her escape, forcing herself to ignore their pleas to let them explain.

Tomorrow she would be back, but for tonight, she needed to be alone. She needed time to rebuild the wall that she hadn't needed for over two years.

A wall she promised herself she would never be without again.

Chapter Two

Jesse ignored yet another ring of her cell phone, waiting until it stopped again to turn it off.

She'd already called her sister, Nat, and promised to call her again once she stopped for the night. The other calls all came from Clay and Rio, and she couldn't handle talking to them while she drove.

She knew they'd expect her to head north to Tulsa, or that she would be contrary and head south. So, she went west.

She wouldn't put it past them to have the police looking for her car, the new one they'd bought her after her old one kept breaking down.

To be safe, she stayed on back roads, not stopping until she found a large economy hotel, hoping she would blend in. The parking lot was crowded, probably due more to the bar connected to it than to the hotel itself.

Thankful that her mind started to clear and she remembered she still carried the money from the store register in her purse, she checked in without having to use her credit card. Clay and Rio probably had the town sheriff, Ace Tyler, monitoring her credit card, waiting for her to use it somewhere.

As soon as she put the *do not disturb* sign on the doorknob and locked the door behind her, she tossed her purse on the nightstand next to the bed and went straight to the thermostat, turning the heat on high.

Even though the night had turned cold, the chill she felt now had more to do with nerves and fear than it did with the outside temperature.

She couldn't get over the fact that she'd probably lost the two men she loved more than her own life, men she'd expected to grow old with.

She threw back the bedspread, ripping the blanket from the bed to wrap around herself before rummaging through her purse for her cell phone, which as usual, had fallen to the bottom.

Sitting on the bed cross-legged, she pulled the blanket more tightly around herself and turned the phone on, unsurprised that it rang again before she even had a chance to make a call.

Despite her actions, she'd never been a coward, but mind-numbing fear had made her act like one. Fear made her stupid.

No more.

Seeing Clay's cell number on the display, she pushed the button to answer and, with shaking hands, lifted the phone to her ear.

"I was just about to call you. Look, I'm sorry I ran out that way."

"Jesse! Thank God."

The fear and relief in Clay's deep voice couldn't be mistaken. Closing her eyes, she blinked back tears, the rip to her heart letting her know that she still had a lot more work to do on the wall she'd begun to rebuild before she could even think about facing them again.

"I just wanted to let you know that I'm okay."

"You're not okay, and I don't have a fucking clue why."

Jesse had to swallow the lump in her throat before speaking. "I just didn't want you to worry."

* * * *

Clay wanted nothing more than to hold his wife in his arms and comfort her, to feel her soft and warm against him so he knew she was safe. With a warning look at his brother, Rio, to keep his temper to himself, he put the phone on speaker.

"Of course we're worried about you, baby. Please, just tell us where you are so we can come and get you."

"No, Clay." The trembling sob in her voice tore him up inside.

With his heart in his throat, he turned, meeting the cold, hard stare of Lucas Hart, one of the partners in Desire Security Systems—and more than that—a good friend.

Lucas had been giving him dirty looks since they'd arrived a little more than an hour ago, clearly blaming Clay and Rio for hurting Jesse.

Clay blamed himself even more.

He'd hoped, prayed, that Jesse would answer the phone and that Lucas could use some of his vast array of equipment to find her.

Clenching his jaw, Lucas motioned for Clay to keep Jesse talking.

Clay had no intention of letting Jesse hang up, especially after spending the last few hours out of his mind with worry.

"Jesse, what do you mean, no? What happened, honey? We don't even know what's wrong. It's not like you not to talk to us. If you're mad at us for something, I'd rather you just give us hell like you usually do. It's not like you to run away."

"I guess you're tired of having a woman who stands up for herself." She said it in such a low voice that Clay almost missed it, but she continued on before he could say anything.

"I'll be back tomorrow. I just need to be alone tonight."

"You don't need to be alone. You need to be with us!" Clay winced inwardly as the knot in his stomach turned to ice.

He kept his voice low, struggling to speak calmly when he was anything but. "You said you'll be *back* tomorrow. You didn't say you were coming *home*. You're scaring the hell out of me, Jesse. If you think I'm letting you go, you're very much mistaken. Just talk to us. Let me explain."

Her silence scared him, and for several heart-stopping seconds, he feared she'd hung up. When she spoke again, the weariness and distance in her tone frightened him even more.

"Clay, I really don't want to talk about this tonight. I've got to go—"

"No. Don't you hang up on me, Jesse Erickson!" He scrubbed a hand over his face, praying that Lucas would be able to pinpoint her location before she hung up. Worry for her ate him alive.

"Baby? Are you cold? You left without your coat. Please tell me you're someplace warm, honey."

The sob in her sigh tore at him, the effect also apparent on both Rio and Lucas as they listened.

Rio sank into a chair, hanging his head, his hair mussed from running his hands through it countless times in the last few hours.

A muscle worked in Lucas's jaw, his steely gaze holding Clay's and his stonelike expression even harder and more intimidating than ever.

Jesse's voice, so sweet and with a tremble in it that brought another lump to Clay's throat, came over the speaker, softer now than before.

"I'm fine, Clay. I'm a big girl, remember? I'm not one of those sweet little things that fall all over you. I'm used to taking care of myself, or have you forgotten?"

The reminder of the cold, withdrawn woman he'd met two years earlier, a woman that had thought herself incapable of loving or being loved, nearly took him to his knees.

"I haven't forgotten a single thing about you."

The ice in his stomach seemed to spread, making him cold all the way to the bone and stiff with fear.

Her tone, a tone he'd never hoped to hear again, sounded so much like the one she'd used when he'd first met her that his heart skipped a beat and he actually felt dizzy for a moment.

Losing Jesse would kill him.

He didn't even try to keep his frustration and fear out of his voice, hoping to get through to her.

He *had* to get through to her.

"Jesse, of course I'm worried about you. You're my wife. You disappeared into the night without no coat and no dinner. I'm sure you didn't eat anything. I know you, baby. When you're upset, Rio and I have to practically force you to eat. That means you're cold and hungry and I can't get to you to make you eat, or to keep you warm. You're hurting and I can't hold you."

His arms ached to hold her close.

"Please tell me where you are, Jesse. We need to talk, to straighten this out. I can't stop thinking about the way you looked at me." That look of confusion and hurt in her eyes would haunt him forever.

Jesse's choked sigh cut his heart to shreds. "We'll talk, Clay. Tomorrow. Look, I'm sorry I acted like a coward and ran off that way, but it was such a shock. I've been stupid and never saw it coming. I should have paid more attention. I should have realized that you felt neglected."

Her voice lowered, so low he had trouble hearing her.

"I've always suspected it would end some day. I knew better. I just thought I would see it coming."

"What?" Clay barked into the phone, whirling to meet Rio's eyes. The half-crazed look in his brother's eyes probably mirrored his own, and he would bet anything his brother's insides twisted with the same agony his did. He swallowed heavily, sick with nausea at the fact that she really *had* assumed that one day he and Rio would fall out of love with her.

Didn't she realize they'd spent a lifetime waiting for her?

"Jesse, are you out of your fucking mind?" He ignored Lucas's warning glare, knowing damned well how to talk to his wife without anyone else's advice.

"Damn it, Jesse, I'm not interested in anyone but you. Jesus, Jesse, I thought you knew by now how Rio and I both feel about you."

"Yeah, I thought I did, too. Listen, I don't want to get into this now, but I heard you and Rio talking in the kitchen. I heard you say that you knew I didn't suspect anything and that I believed you when you lied to me about being at the club. I heard you say you were meeting someone, obviously someone you didn't want me to know about. I've been so busy worried about Jake and Nat that I didn't even think to wonder about us. I was so stupid."

Clay dropped into one of the leather chairs in front of Lucas's desk, reliving the anger and disillusionment he'd experienced when he'd overheard and misunderstood one of Jesse's phone conversations shortly after they'd first met.

At that time he'd been sure it was over between them. The knowledge that Jesse now believed the same made him feel as if his insides had been ripped out.

He knew her well, but had become so used to hearing her voice filled with happiness, that he felt now as if he spoke to a stranger.

Her voice broke. "Clay, you sounded so serious and so torn. We both know you wouldn't lie to me unless there was a good reason. For you to be so upset and still meet her, it could only mean one thing. You can't stay away from her. You're in love."

Clay wanted to smash something. "Damn it, Jesse. I love *you*! There's no other fucking woman!"

Jesse blew out a breath and he pictured her looking up at the ceiling and blinking back tears.

"I can't get my head around this right now. I just wanted you to know I'm okay. I'll be back tomorrow. I just need a little time alone to think and to get my bearings back."

On a sob, she disconnected before Clay could stop her.

Rio rubbed his eyes before turning his head to meet Clay's eyes. "We haven't spent a single night apart since we got married. I don't think I could ever sleep without her next to me. How the hell could she think we could ever be involved with another woman?"

Clay sighed, forcing himself to relax his hold on the phone before he crushed it in his hands. He needed it in case Jesse called.

"She heard us talking about meeting Jake, only somehow Jesse thinks it was a woman we were meeting. Hell, I don't even remember what we said, but she figured that if we were lying to her and meeting someone behind her back, it had to be a woman."

Lucas came to his feet, reaching for the jacket he'd hooked over the back of his chair. He came around his desk and touched Rio's shoulder. "Well, you won't have to be without your wife tonight. I've got her location. She's about three hours west of here. I'll go with you to make sure she hasn't moved, and drive her car back. I'm sure you both want to be alone with her."

Clay headed for the door, anxious to get to his wife. "Damned right. Thanks, Lucas. I appreciate this. I don't know what we would have done if you hadn't been able to find her. I can't imagine what tonight would have been like if all we could do was sit around and wait. I'm not good at doing nothing."

Lucas nodded, his expression grim. "Well, you'll have three hours to figure out how the hell to get Jesse back. Everyone loves her and I wouldn't want to be in your shoes if she leaves."

Clay winced at the thought, the knots in his stomach so tight he wanted to vomit.

"I wouldn't want to be in my own shoes. I couldn't live without her, Lucas."

* * * *

So nervous he couldn't sit still, Rio shifted in his seat again, unable to find a comfortable position. Each mile they drove seemed to take forever, the need to get to Jesse as soon as possible making him jittery.

"I can't believe Jesse could even think we'd ever be involved with someone else. Christ, that woman is everything to me!" Rio stuck out a hand in front of him. "I'm so fucking mad and scared I'm shaking."

Hearing Lucas speaking from the backseat into his cell phone to one of his partners, Rio glanced at Clay. "What the hell's in that head of hers? Haven't we told her, *shown* her how much we love her every fucking day?"

Clay's jaw tightened, barely visible in the low light of the dashboard. "I thought so. I can't imagine what the hell we did wrong. I knew sometimes she was insecure about us, but I would never have believed she would fly off the handle that way. If she overheard something that made her suspicious, she should have talked to us. Hell, she's never had trouble keeping us on our toes before."

The self-anger in Clay's thoughtful tone made him feel even worse. Clenching his fists on his lap, Rio stared out the window, his anger growing by the minute.

"Look at this. It's so dark, you can't see a thing." Squinting against the approaching headlights, he cursed.

"Hardly any traffic. Nothing around for miles."

Clay cursed through gritted teeth. "And Jesse drove this in the dark. If she'd had any car trouble…"

Disconnecting from a call to one of his partners, Lucas leaned forward.

"I'm glad you bought her that new car. The other one was a real piece of junk. You might want to think about letting me hook up a GPS system to it now."

Rio half turned in his seat. "Do it. When you take her car, hook it up, and let us know when we can come pick it up. I can't go through this again."

Clay attempted to laugh, but it fell short. "I can only imagine the kind of shit you and the others will have hooked up to your woman."

Lucas sighed. "If we're ever lucky enough to find a woman like yours, we're sure as hell going to make sure she's safe. She won't get a chance to take off like this. If she even tries it, I'll turn her over my knee and make sure she doesn't sit down for a week."

Rio turned to stare in the distance, using his anger to keep the terror at bay.

"Yeah, well good luck with that."

Despite her larger-than-life spirit, and her ability to handle herself in most situations, Jesse was still a woman, and seemed so delicate and fragile to him.

She'd called both of them overprotective and chauvinistic many times in the last two years. He couldn't deny it, and couldn't be any other way with her. She was his world, and the thought of anything happening to her scared the hell out of him.

She was his life, and had been since the moment he'd first laid eyes on her.

One look.

One touch.

It had been as simple, and as complicated as that as he realized almost immediately that he'd found the woman he'd spent a lifetime searching for.

"God. No!"

Jolted from his thoughts by Clay's horror-filled shout, Rio followed his brother's gaze, and felt his entire world crumble around him.

The curses pouring from Lucas seemed to come from a great distance as his mind went numb.

Unable to tear his gaze away from the terrifying sight in the distance, Rio braced himself with a hand on the door and one on the dashboard as Clay drove like a madman toward the horror.

Clay cursed soundly. "Lucas, please tell me that's not Jesse's hotel."

Lucas cursed. "It is. Clay, for God's sake, don't wreck before we can get to her."

When they pulled into the parking lot several heart-pounding seconds later, Rio jumped out of the truck before they'd even come to a stop, racing toward the burning two-story building. He screamed his wife's name in a voice filled with horror and desperation, whipping his head around frantically for any sign of her.

Nothing in his life had ever been as important as getting to her. If anything happened to Jesse, he didn't know how he would go on.

Racing toward the fire, he ignored the shouts from all around him, caring about nothing but dragging her from the flames.

With a hand over his mouth and nose, he started into the burning building, pausing when he saw a flash of red from the second floor.

Jesse!

Chapter Three

Jesse couldn't stand the noise anymore. She'd turned on the television for some background sound in the too-quiet room, but now it just got on her nerves. With jerky movements, she turned it off and tossed the remote aside, groaning when she heard the loud voices and music coming from the bar downstairs.

She'd been told at check-in that the hotel was hosting a convention, and it sounded as if the seminars had finished for the day. It appeared the partygoers from the bar had moved some of the party out to the parking lot.

Now, the noise came from right below her window.

She started toward the phone to call the manager, and almost immediately decided against it. She stopped with her hand on the receiver, lifting it again as she sank down on the bed and pulled the blanket tighter. She wouldn't be getting any sleep tonight anyway, and figured it would be a shame to ruin their fun.

The thought of how much she could be enjoying tonight had her blinking back tears. It seemed impossible that only a few hours ago, she'd been happy and secure in a marriage she valued above all else.

In a matter of minutes, everything had changed.

Now that the shock had passed and her mind began to clear, she began to see that there had to be some sort of an explanation. She considered calling, but she needed to see their faces when she spoke to them again.

She had to have misunderstood something. If Clay and Rio didn't love her, or want her anymore, she would have known it.

She would have *felt* it.

No. She couldn't believe it was over between them. Something had to be terribly wrong.

That something was her.

It had been a shock to her that she'd fallen apart that way, but her sister's marriage problems had made her even more insecure than she'd realized. Because of it, she'd been quick to believe the worst, something that pissed her off immensely.

She would go back tomorrow and give Clay and Rio a chance to explain, but first she had to make peace with herself and deal with her own issues.

Neither Clay nor Rio had ever been shy about expressing their feelings, and neither one of them ever did anything in half measures.

If they had something to say to her, they would have said it.

Sneaking around had never been their style.

Both men had always been hard and outspoken, and honest to a fault.

Shaking her head, she couldn't hold back a smile. Those qualities had always been what she loved most about them.

She relaxed just a little, but knew she wouldn't relax more until she spoke to them, and it would be a long time before she relaxed completely.

She'd learned something about herself that had shaken her to her core.

Clay and Rio had obviously been lying to her about something, and she'd take that up with them as soon as she got back home, but her own reaction to it and swift leap to believe they'd found someone else really shook her.

She'd thought herself stronger than that, but just the thought of losing them had nearly destroyed her.

Coming to her feet, she reached for her phone again to look at the time. Surprised to see that it was already almost two in the morning, she paused, wondering if she should start back tonight.

She wouldn't be getting any sleep anyway, and if she waited until morning to start back, she would be even more tired.

Having made her decision, she wanted to get out of here and get back to Desire as soon as possible.

Tossing off the blanket, she reached for her purse, pausing when she smelled smoke. Thinking it might have to do with the party downstairs, she went to the window and jerked the curtains aside, her heart dropping when she saw nothing but thick smoke and the lick of flames off to her left.

Hearing screams and shouts from below, she struggled to see through the smoke, but saw nothing but an occasional glow from below. Panicked now, she raced to the door, relieved to find it cool.

With shaking hands, she adjusted her purse, fitting the strap over her head to keep it secure in front of her before unlocking the door. She opened it slowly, inch by inch, and seeing the raging fire, sucked in a breath, regretting it almost immediately as smoke filled her room and she began coughing.

This couldn't be happening.

Tears filled her eyes, tears from the smoke mingling with tears of fear that she would never see her husbands or their sons ever again.

Panicked people raced all around her, and she had to hold on to the railing to keep her balance as she turned right in an attempt to make her way to the front of the building, away from the flames.

The smoke seemed to get thicker, the breeze blowing the smoke and flames toward her.

"Jesse!"

Still coughing, Jesse stopped, turning toward the frantic voice coming from somewhere to her left and below her. Deciding she must have been hallucinating, she hurried along the now-deserted walkway, holding the neckline of her red sweater over her mouth and nose in a desperate attempt to escape the smoke.

The roar of the flames just seemed to get louder. Several people shouted, and when sirens approached, the noise became deafening.

Still, she could swear she heard her name called from several different directions, the voices becoming louder and more frantic by the second.

It almost sounded like Clay and Rio, but that would have been impossible.

More tears ran down her cheeks. Her longing to be with them had become so strong she imagined their voices calling her.

She could hear nothing then over the sound of the fire truck, but when the engine stopped, she heard it again.

"Jesse, damn it! Where are you?"

Rio!

This time the voice came from almost directly below her.

She slid the neckline of her sweater down. "Rio?" The smoke forced her to pull it back up again.

"Jesse? Clay! Lucas! Over here."

A gust of wind blew enough of the smoke away for her to see his face.

His beloved face.

He looked frantic, his eyes wild with worry for her.

Pulling the neck of her sweater lower, Jesse gasped, and began coughing again. Through it, she tried to speak, her voice coming out as a croak.

"Rio! What are you doing here?"

"Are you crazy? What do you think I'm doing here? Jump, baby. I'll catch you."

The wind shifted and she could no longer see him. "Rio?"

"I'm here, baby. Jump."

"I can't see you!"

She had to pull the sweater back up as the smoke thickened again.

"The stairs are gone, Jesse. I'll catch you. Jump, baby. Trust me."

Before she even realized she meant to, she lifted one foot over the railing, cursing when her hand slipped on it and she almost toppled over. She pushed her purse out of the way and grabbed on tight, one leg on one side of the cold, wet metal and one on the other. "Rio, the railing's all wet and slippery. Damn it, I'm gonna fall."

"Would I let that happen? I'm right here, darlin'. I'll catch you."

She heard the tension in his voice, even though he tried to disguise it. She knew him too well to be fooled by it.

She knew him too well to be fooled.

She also trusted him with her life.

With one foot braced on the bottom of the outside of the railing, she lifted her other over the top, wincing at the feel of the hard metal pressing into her ribs.

"Rio, if you drop me, I swear I'm going to kick your ass."

Another voice sounded from below her, one equally beloved and filled with anger, fear, and relief.

"So will I. Jump, Jesse. Right now."

The sounds around her faded somewhat as she concentrated on the voices of her husbands, squinting to catch a glimpse of them in the heavy smoke.

Holding herself away from the railing with the toes of her sneakers pressed hard against the concrete, Jesse looked down over her shoulder.

"I'm letting go. Don't you dare drop me."

"Not a chance, darlin'. Let go."

With a cry, Jesse closed her eyes tight and released her grip on the railing, her fall stopped abruptly when she landed in a pair of strong, muscular arms, arms she knew so well.

"Gotcha!"

Nestled against Rio's wide chest, she opened her eyes and began to cough again, nearly crushed to death against him as he breathed her name. "Jesse. Thank God. You're never leaving my sight again."

He spun and started moving fast, but with her eyes closed, she didn't see where they were going.

She didn't care. She'd never found anyplace safer than Rio and Clay's arms.

Clay moved in on her other side, taking a wet cloth from someone standing behind him and slapping it over her mouth and nose. "Thank God. Keep this over your face, baby."

The familiar endearment both men used warmed her inside, and she found herself relaxing a little more.

Everything would be all right. It had to be.

Once they'd moved away from the smoke, Jesse took the damp cloth from her face and gripped Rio's shoulder.

"I love you, Rio. I was leaving to come home. I don't know what's going on, but I need the truth from you and Clay. I can't go on without it."

Rio shook his head, his jaw tightening. "I hate keeping things from you, but you deserve to be put over my knee for thinking we'd ever cheat on you."

More of the tension eased, and she wrapped her arms around his neck, hugging him close. "You try it and you'll be sorry."

Reaching the paramedics, Rio set her on her feet, holding her as Clay wrapped his arms around her from behind.

Clay buried his face against her neck, breathing deeply. "Peaches and Jesse. Christ, honey, you scared the hell out of me. Are you hurt anywhere?"

"No." Waving away the paramedic's attempts to tend to her, she blinked in surprise, pointing toward the bar where the fire appeared to be almost out. "Is that Lucas over there? Why the hell is Lucas here? What's going on?"

Rio led her to the patient paramedic, holding her while the other man tended to the scratches on her hands she hadn't even been aware of.

"He helped us find you. He's over there probably getting the whole story of what happened here. Be still, honey. Lucas is going to drive your car home while you come home in the truck with us."

Clay stood stone-faced, his arms crossed over his chest and his hooded eyes sharp as he watched the paramedic clean and bandage her scratches.

Rio kept rubbing her arm, his fingers closing around it each time she moved as if making sure she didn't get away from him.

Jerking her arm from his hold, she glared at him. "Let go of me. If I want to go, I'll go. I said I was going back to Desire to talk to you and I was. I'm not going anywhere until I hear some answers from both of you."

She knew both of them well enough to know how possessive and angry they were, but she couldn't let that sway her. Poking her finger into Clay's massive chest, she let him see her own anger.

"Don't you give me that look. You lied to me, remember?"

Clay ran his hand over her hair, pulling her close. "Yes, but you should know that we'd never look at another woman, and you sure as hell know better than to run away. Damn it, Jesse. You should have talked to us."

She glanced at the paramedic, yanking her hand away as soon as he finished bandaging her. "I couldn't."

Lucas came rushing back. "Hey, honey." He frowned when he saw the bandages on her hands. "She okay?"

Jesse gritted her teeth. "I can speak for myself, Lucas. I'm fine."

Lucas nodded, not looking convinced, sharing one of those looks with Clay and Rio that the men in Desire were so famous for.

"Bar fight. It carried outside, bottles were thrown and people were smoking. I told them she was safe, and that we're leaving. Jesse, where was your room?"

Jesse turned. "Above the bar. Right over there." She pointed, her jaw dropping when she saw what had once been her room. "Oh, my God! It's gone."

Clay gripped her arm. "Give Lucas your car keys. Let's get the hell out of here. I can't take any more tonight."

Chapter Four

Clay glanced at his wife, his body shaking with the need to take her, and with fear at how close he'd come to losing her.

He'd wanted her since the first time he'd laid eyes on her, and time had done nothing to diminish that.

Familiarity only made him want her more.

The desperation and the hunger for her now made him feel like a caged tiger. He wanted to sink so deep inside her that she never again forgot for one minute that she belonged to him. He needed to feel her all around him, to satisfy himself that she was all right.

He'd have nightmares about tonight for years.

Jesse shifted in her seat. "You wanted to talk. Talk."

Clay forced a calm into his voice he didn't feel. "No, Jesse. The conversation we're going to have deserves my full attention, something I can't give you while I'm driving. When we get home, we'll talk."

"But you can't drive all the way home! It's too far. Why don't we stop and—"

Clay gritted his teeth, surprising himself by growling. "We're going home. I'm wide awake, Jesse. Believe me. Didn't you tell me just a few minutes ago that you were going to drive home tonight instead of calling us to come get you?"

Just the thought of it made his stomach clench. "You need to be spanked more often." The thought of turning his sweet wife over his lap had his cock demanding attention. Blowing out a breath, he fought it. "You're safe now. Why don't you get some sleep?"

He sure as hell needed a few hours to settle.

"Look, Clay, I don't need you or Rio to come get me when I'm perfectly—"

His stomach churned, rage at how close he'd come to losing her spewing. "Don't even start, Jesse. You do *not* want to have this conversation with me right now. Just go to sleep before I give in to the urge to pull over and paddle your ass raw!"

Jesse whirled in her seat. "Listen, you son of a bitch, I—"

With a hand wrapped around her waist, Rio yanked her back against him, overcoming her struggles. "I wouldn't, if I were you. Just settle down and go to sleep. We're all on edge right now."

To Clay's relief, Jesse complied, but not before grumbling under her breath and giving both of them dirty looks. He knew he and Rio would pay for snapping at her later, but right now, he only wanted to concentrate on driving and getting his wife back home where she belonged.

He also needed to calm down before they talked. In his present mood, he didn't know what the hell he would say.

No one spoke, the cab of the truck silent except for the monotonous sound of the engine, and before long, Jesse slumped against Rio. Without saying a word, Rio gathered her against him, the hand he placed on her shoulder holding her close.

Neither one of them had been able to keep their hands off of her since they'd found her, and Clay knew it would be a long time before he would be able to relax his guard again.

She'd scared him badly, given him the kind of scare he wouldn't forget soon.

Glancing at his brother, he rubbed Jesse's thigh, careful to keep his voice low. "We'll work it out with her tomorrow. We can't tell her everything, but we'll tell her enough. She's back with us, and right now, that's all that matters."

Rio nodded, burying his face in Jesse's hair. "Yeah. She's with us." Staring down at her, he sighed. "We all smell like smoke, but I can still smell the peach lotion she wears."

Clay glanced at him, clenching his jaw. "Seems like such a stupid thing, but some of the knots in my stomach loosened when I breathed it in. Ridiculous."

Closing his eyes, Rio pulled the jacket he'd covered her with higher over her shoulder. "Stupid." Sitting up slightly, he stared down at her again, playing with the ends of her hair.

"She's been waiting for it, hasn't she? She's been waiting for us to tell her it's over."

With a sigh, Clay glanced at her again. "Yes, she has, and it pisses me off."

Nodding again, Rio dropped his head back against the headrest and stared out the windshield, still playing with Jesse's hair.

"I won't lose her."

Clay clenched his jaw, almost smiling at the determination in his brother's voice. "That's not an option. The boys are away and Nat's taking care of the store. We'll have Jesse all to ourselves this weekend, and we'll get this settled once and for all."

Rio curled his hand over Jesse's small hand resting on his thigh. "I wonder sometimes if she really gets it—if she realizes what the word *wife* means to the men in Desire. What it means to *us*."

Clay moved his hand up his wife's leg, smiling for the first time in hours when Jesse moaned in her sleep and arched into his touch.

"She'll know for sure before this weekend's over."

* * * *

Jesse woke slowly, not bothering to open her eyes. As she did every morning, she took the time to savor the warmth and feel of her husbands lying on either side of her.

It had become a precious time for her, this special closeness before the rush of the day started just to be with her men. It had become a ritual for them, and she wouldn't have given this time up for anything.

Nothing else seemed as important as the intimacy in the early-morning quiet, and by unspoken agreement, they always kept their voices low, increasing the intimacy.

Smiling to herself, she shifted her position slightly, smiling again when the hands both Clay and Rio held her with moved, caressing her as if their need to comfort her extended into their sleep.

Wrinkling her nose against the smell of smoke, Jesse gasped, jolting upright as memories of the previous night came rushing back, the feeling of warmth dissipating in a heartbeat.

Rio tightened the arm around her waist, pulling her back down between them again.

"Where do you think you're going?"

The steel in his otherwise drowsy tone set her teeth on edge. "Don't take that tone with me, Rio. I'm still mad at you."

Before she knew it, Jesse found herself flat on her back with Rio's considerable weight pressing her into the mattress.

The feel of his big, hard body against hers never failed to both excite and comfort her, wrapping her in a protective cocoon that nothing could get past. A wall of solid muscle held her closely and moved erotically against her softer curves.

Her nipples burned against his chest, the need to have his attention there nearly unbearable.

It had been this way with both of them since she'd met them.

One touch and she melted.

She couldn't ignore the huge cock pressing against her thigh, and as Clay rolled toward her, she moaned as another hard cock pressed insistently against her hip. She had to fight the urge to spread her thighs wider in invitation, an invitation she knew neither one of them would ignore.

They seemed to find her irresistible, and she'd never quite understood it—or gotten used to it.

No one had ever loved her the way Clay and Rio appeared to, and it left her feeling unsettled at times—something too good to be believed.

It left a small place empty inside her, a small corner of her heart that uncertainty wouldn't allow to be filled.

She'd never minded, and hardly even thought about it anymore, but last night it had taken over, grown so large that she fell into the dark chasm and was unable to breathe until she found her way out.

Staring up at Rio, she lifted her hand, unable to resist pushing back the dark hair that fell rakishly over his forehead.

"I need a shower. Alone."

Love shone in his dark eyes, something she'd come to rely on, but this time his gaze also held a cautious expectancy.

Meeting his eyes, she winced inwardly at the emotional distance between them now, a distance she'd never thought to experience.

Even the hand he used to push her hair back moved with a hesitancy that was so unlike him that she wanted to cry.

Clay leaned over her from the other side, his eyes sharper than usual at this time of the morning.

"Take your shower." Nodding once, he glanced at Rio. "We'll get ours in the other bathroom and meet you in the kitchen." Reaching out, he ran a finger down her cheek, his eyes narrowing when she shivered.

"Don't even think about leaving this house, though."

Jesse sighed, feeling cold as Rio moved aside and slid from the bed in a graceful movement she couldn't help but admire.

"I'm not going anywhere. Both of you owe me some answers." She sat up and scooted toward the edge of the bed.

Hooking an arm around her waist from behind, Clay yanked her back, his breath warm on her ear. "And you owe us an explanation for that foolish stunt last night. Go get your shower. We'll talk when you're done."

Reaching a hand around her to cover a breast, he ran his thumb over her nipple. "You respond so eagerly no matter how mad you are, don't you, honey?"

The sensation, so erotic and familiar, sent a wave of longing through her that couldn't be contained.

Arching into his caress, Jesse let her head fall back against his shoulder with a moan as erotic heat licked at her nipples.

Clay chuckled from behind her. "You think you can walk away from this, baby?"

Furious at her body's betrayal, Jesse turned to glare at him over her shoulder.

"Sex isn't everything."

Clay's brow went up as he increased the pressure on her nipple, sending white-hot flames of need through her. "But, it's never been just sex between us, has it, Jesse?"

Gripping his muscular forearm, Jesse rubbed her thighs together against the flash of heat to her slit.

"Damn it, Clay. We need to talk."

A muscle worked in his jaw. "You're damned right we do. Go get your shower." Releasing her, he rolled to his feet. Reaching back for her, he gripped her upper arms and dragged her from the bed, setting her on her feet in front of him.

"I wouldn't bother getting dressed. You won't be going anywhere until we get this sorted out, and if I have my way, you'll be naked and under me for a long time afterward."

Chapter Five

Tightening the belt of her thick robe, Jesse made her way down the hall to the kitchen. Although she wore thick socks and knew she hadn't made a sound, both men turned as soon as she crossed the threshold.

They'd always been attuned to her somehow, as she had to them.

Butterflies took flight in her stomach, and every erogenous zone came to life as soon as she saw them. Felt them.

The tension in the air this morning, however, made it worse.

Stopping at the doorway, she rubbed her hands up and down her arms and took a few moments to admire her gorgeous husbands, gauging their moods. She let her gaze wander over their muscular physiques, her body shimmering with awareness as their gazes ran over her.

Their bodies, hard from the physical labor, seemed even stiffer now, as though braced for anything.

Both men looked almost haggard from lack of sleep and tension.

"You both look terrible. Did you sleep at all?"

Clay's hooded eyes stayed on hers as she stepped into the room, searching her features as though trying to read her mind. He leaned back against the counter, sipping his coffee as he did every morning, but unlike every other morning, she didn't go to him. If she did, he would have set his coffee aside and wrapped his arms around her, holding her close for a few more precious moments before they started their day.

Rio would bring her a cup of coffee and yank her chair close to his, nuzzling her neck as she drank it.

It had become a routine somehow, and she treasured it, and felt the loss deeply.

Tightening her hands over the back of the chair in front of her, she studied their expressions, seeing the same loss in their eyes.

Clay took another sip of coffee. "When we got home, we stripped you and ourselves and went to bed. No, I didn't sleep much."

Rio's usual morning grin was conspicuously absent as he brought her a cup of coffee, another sharp reminder of the differences between this morning and all the others.

Forcing a smile, she accepted the cup, knowing that he would have fixed it the way she liked it.

"Thank you."

Rio's gaze slid lower, lingering at the opening of her robe, his attention making her nipples bead tighter and ache with the need to be touched. "You're welcome." He smiled, one of those dangerously wicked smiles that always made her heart race, but they danced in a way that alarmed her now more than usual.

"You're very lucky you're not facedown over my knee with your bare ass wiggling on my lap after the stunt you pulled last night."

Tightening her thighs together against the sharp pang of need, Jesse took a sip of her coffee before lowering herself into one of the kitchen chairs. Curling a foot around the leg of it, she eyed him over the rim of her cup, swallowing heavily and wary of his mood.

Raising a brow, she met his gaze squarely, hoping he didn't see the effect his threat had on her. "You're very lucky I didn't knee you in the balls this morning when I had the chance, and put you out of business."

Not appearing the least bit intimidated, Rio reached out a hand, tracing the opening of her robe with the backs of his fingers. His eyes glittered with hunger as his fingertips trailed over the curve of her breast barely an inch from her nipple.

"It wouldn't make any difference. I could fuck you anywhere at any time. My cock is hard anytime I'm with you and at least a dozen times a day when I think about you. The thought of spanking that beautiful ass of yours is all that kept me from losing my mind last night."

Gathering the lapels of her robe together in one strong hand, he pulled her close. "I never stop wanting you. I'll want you until I die."

Staring into her eyes, he smiled humorlessly and released her. "And for some reason, that surprises you. Amazing."

Fighting back a moan at the sharp tingling in her nipples, Jesse wrapped both hands around her cup to warm them and to hide the fact that they shook. Desire flooded through her veins, and part of her wanted to forget the talk and go back to bed, to reestablish the connection between them in the most basic way possible.

It would only be temporary, however, tainted with the knowledge that they still had issues to face.

Swallowing the lump in her throat, she lifted her head, meeting their eyes squarely.

"You lied to me."

Clay set his cup aside and approached, turning her chair and kneeling in front of her. "We did, but you took off without letting us explain."

Rio dropped into the seat on the other side of her, turning his chair and sliding it closer to settle in right behind her. "We kept a secret from you, but it was nothing that deserved that. I know we had a misunderstanding when we first met you and that neither one of us gave you a chance to explain then. But, honey, that was a long time ago and we didn't have what we have now."

Wrapping his arms around her from behind, he rubbed his cheek against her hair. "We're dealing with a bigger issue here than a small lie, aren't we, Jesse?"

Clay ran his hands over her thighs, the heat from them making her pussy clench with anticipation.

"An issue we need to address. You really shook us up, baby."

She knew their touch, and the pleasure that followed. She knew that if this had been any other morning, Clay's hands would have been under her robe instead of over it.

They always seemed to be touching her.

They'd learned her body well over the last two years and used that knowledge to arouse her every time they had a chance.

Her thighs shook with the effort it cost her to sit still, so she straightened her leg, placing both feet on the floor. She couldn't allow herself to show any sign of weakness, at least until she got the answers she needed. Shaking so hard that coffee sloshed over the side of her cup, she set it carefully on the table and unwrapped her hands from it, pushing it aside before meeting their eyes.

"Don't think you're going to change the subject. Where were you going when you told me you were going to the club? You said I didn't suspect anything and you wanted to keep it that way. Who were you meeting with? What did you mean when you said that I felt things too strongly? Am I smothering you? Have you decided you made a mistake? Do you want a divorce?"

Clay's jaw clenched. "That mind of yours has been really busy thinking the worst."

Rio cursed, lifting her from her seat as he stood and gathered her against him, sitting again with her on his lap. When she tried to get up, he merely knocked her off-balance, catching her when she fell against him. "That's better." Taking her hand in his, he waited until Clay took the seat Jesse had been sitting in and turned it, effectively surrounding her.

She stiffened, recognizing the look in their eyes. "Damn it, Rio. Stop it. We have to talk."

Ignoring her protest, he slipped his hand inside her robe, closing it over her breast. "We were meeting Jake at his store after closing. You know he and Nat have had some issues and Jake wanted to talk."

Jesse opened her mouth to ask what the hell was going on that made her sister so unhappy, but Rio put a finger to her lips, shaking his head.

"No. We're not going to tell you what he wanted to talk about, which is why we didn't tell you we were meeting with him to begin with. It's between them. Nat talks to you and we don't ask questions, and Jake feels comfortable talking to us. He just needs someone to talk to. This thing with Nat is eating him up inside and there's nothing he can do about it right now."

Clay sighed, slipping his hand under the hem of her robe, his eyes watchful. "We don't like keeping secrets from you, but we didn't think it was worth us fighting about, so we didn't tell you."

Jesse raised a brow, shifting restlessly on Rio's lap as Clay's hand moved higher, her abdomen clenching as a rush of moisture dampened her thighs. "Especially after you told me to stay out of it and then got involved in it yourself?"

Clay slid his hand higher, a ghost of a smile playing at his lips when she gasped. "He's our brother-in-law, Jesse, and we've been friends for years. We've been worried about both of them, but we didn't want you to. You've been making yourself sick worrying about Nat, and with being overworked at the store, you've been under a lot of stress. I don't like it."

Jesse bristled at his arrogance, but her insides began to relax.

"I'm a big girl. I can handle the store, and of course I'm worried about Nat. She's my sister, and she's not happy. Is Jake cheating on her?"

Clay frowned. "Of course not, and that's all I'm telling you. It'll work out for them one way or another."

Jesse sat up, crying out at Rio's tug to her nipple, and the answering sharp pull to her clit. "What do you mean, one way or another? Is there a chance they might get divorced?"

The thought of it scared her to death. Her sister adored her husband, and Jesse had always thought Jake adored her. Her sister and brother-in-law had always seemed so close, touching each other all the time and sharing intimate looks that shut out the rest of the world—looks that Jesse now shared with Clay and Rio.

It scared her that they seemed so distant now.

With the hand cupping her breast, Rio nudged her back, draping her over his arm, the look in his eyes reminding her that she had her own issues to deal with right now.

Running his hands over her, Rio smiled. "I don't think either one of them will let that happen. They love each other, don't they?"

Jesse nodded. "Of course, but—"

Clay slid his hand higher up her thigh, his fingers dancing erotically over her bare mound. From the very beginning, they'd insisted she keep her mound waxed, something that seemed to give all three of them a great deal of pleasure.

"Enough. This is why we didn't tell you anything about meeting with Jake. You have enough to worry about. I would rather talk about why you were in such a hurry to jump to the conclusion that we were cheating on you."

With Rio's fingers teasing a nipple and Clay's moving dangerously close to her clit, Jesse swallowed heavily, struggling to hide the tremors that fluttered under her skin.

"What was I supposed to think when you talked about meeting someone and that I didn't suspect anything? What was that crap about me caring too much? Caring about you? You didn't answer me. Am I smothering you?"

Clay scowled and forced her legs apart. "You couldn't smother me with your love if you tried. I always want all I can get. I would like some trust, though."

Jesse's stomach muscles quivered under Clay's lips, her body trembling helplessly at the feel of his warm lips moving lower to her mound. Holding her breath as he used his thumbs to part her folds, she jolted, going stiff when his hot tongue darted out to touch her clit.

Clay lifted his head, his eyes filled with love, concern, and devious intent as he slid a finger through her slick juices.

"You're always braced for disappointment, aren't you, baby? You still don't trust us enough to let go of that. It's frustrating as hell, you know."

Jesse shrugged and tried to gather her robe around herself, but Rio stopped her. Baring the rest of her and cupping both of her breasts, he ran his thumbs back and forth over her nipples, something that always drove her wild.

She tried to push his hands away, struggling to keep track of the conversation, but couldn't budge them. "Damn it, Rio. Look, Clay, that's my problem. I'm sorry I didn't trust you and—"

Rio chuckled and rolled her nipples between his thumbs and forefingers, increasing the pressure and sending ripples of pleasure to gather at her slit. "How sorry?"

Jesse couldn't hold back a cry, her breath catching when Clay lowered his head, placing a kiss on her mound.

"What? Wh–what do you mean—how sorry? You're the one who lied to me and oh!" Jolting at the slide of Clay's tongue over her sensitive clit, Jesse gripped Rio's forearms, her entire body shaking.

Clay lifted his head slightly, his mouth dangerously close to her slit.

"And we've apologized for that and explained why. We'll do whatever we can to make it up to you, but Jake needs someone to talk to. There isn't, and never will be, another woman."

Rio nuzzled her neck in that sensitive spot they both exploited at every opportunity.

"I thought you knew how much we love you, Jesse. We tell you constantly and I thought we'd shown you just how much you mean to us."

With a sigh, Jesse stiffened, not knowing when or where they would touch her next. "I told you—it's my problem. I overreacted."

She wanted to scream at Clay to finish her off, but she had the feeling that he'd purposely left her poised on the edge.

He moved forward, spreading her thighs wider as he got in her face, his eyes narrowed.

"Tell me what happened last night. Why did you look at us as if we were strangers and take off without even talking to us? You've never had any trouble yelling at us or demanding answers before."

His eyes gentled, the hurt and love in them making her feel like a fool.

"Why, honey? What happened?"

Jesse blinked back tears, trembling helplessly with arousal. "Let me up a minute. Please. I can't think like this."

"No." Clay stared into her eyes while his thumbs caressed her folds, keeping her open to him. "I like you like this."

Jesse moaned, sucking in another breath when Rio tugged her nipples.

"I panicked, okay? I've always believed that saying that if it's too good to be true, it usually is." She took a shuddering breath, her knees shaking. "When all this started happening to Nat, I wondered how long it would take for it to happen to us."

Her words came out in a rush, her breathing ragged. Watching Clay, she tightened her hands on Rio's forearms, her body tight as she waited expectantly for a touch that could come at any moment.

Clay brushed his lips over her mound, his eyes sharp and filled with self-anger. "And you walked in to hear us talking about meeting someone and that you didn't suspect a thing."

"Yes." Now that the crisis had passed, she felt weepy.

"It's my fault, though. I should have stayed and talked to you. I just…couldn't breathe. I couldn't think. I just wanted to get away until I could function again."

Clay straightened and took her in his arms, pulling her against him. Threading a hand into her hair, he tilted her face up for his kiss.

Lust, hot and intoxicating, slammed into her, the desperation in his kiss feeding her own. Her head spun when she felt herself being lifted against him and carried from the room.

Halfway down the hall, he broke off their kiss and lifted his head, the intense possessiveness and need in his eyes making her shiver in reaction.

"It amazes me that after living in Desire for over two years—being married to Rio and me for almost that long—you still don't understand that the word *wife* means something here, Jesse. We don't take women or marriage lightly in Desire."

His deep voice had a gruffness to it, filled with an anger directed at himself that left her staring up at him in shock. It also held more than a hint of pride in the fact that the men in this town took such good care of their women.

A muscle worked in his jaw as he strode into the bedroom and paused next to the bed. He stared down at her, his eyes darker and glittering with raw emotion.

"You know we protect and cherish the women here in Desire, but when that woman is your *wife*—it's more, so much more."

Rio moved in beside her, running his hand up and down her leg, his expression hard, while his eyes swirled with frustration and love. "It's everything. *Everything.* How you can't know that by now is beyond me."

Looking from one to the other, Jesse shook her head. "It's not that. It just hit me so hard and I realized just how empty my life would be without either one of you. I hate feeling so needy."

Clay moved in behind her and loosened the belt of her robe. "We need to be needed." He slid the robe from her shoulders, letting it puddle at her feet.

Bending from his considerable height, Rio brushed his lips over her shoulder as he ran his fingers over her breast, leaving trails of heat behind. "I adore you, Jesse Erickson. You're my world."

Clay stripped off his clothing with a speed that spoke of urgency. "I want you, Jesse. Badly. Words just aren't going to be enough for any of us."

As always, the sight of his nakedness made her heart race.

He stood a foot taller than her own average height, every inch of his body packed tight with muscle. Sexy as hell, he excited her with just a glance, but it had always been the way she felt in his arms that turned her inside out.

Until she met Clay and Rio, she'd never known it could be possible to feel beautiful, feminine, and desired, while feeling so safe and secure in their arms.

Naked, aroused, and with a gleam in his eyes, Clay nudged her, knocking her off-balance to land in the soft bedding. He followed her down, keeping most of his weight off of her while covering her body with his much larger one.

He slid a hand beneath her neck to lift her face to his, his jaw clenched tight, his eyes narrowed to slits.

"Do you have any idea, Jesse Erickson, how much my life's changed since you became my wife?" Sliding a hand under her body, he lifted her against him, his cock hard against her inner thigh.

"Do you know that I look forward to every day now because you're in my life? I live to be with you, Jesse."

Rio, now naked, tossed back the covers on the other side of the bed. Reaching into the nightstand drawer, he retrieved a tube and tossed it by the pillow, the bed shifting as he slid in beside her.

"Only both of us taking you together is going to be enough today, isn't it, darlin'?"

Jesse knew he was right.

Nothing could match the closeness or the passion of having both of her husbands taking her at the same time, the trust and level of intimacy involved unmatched by anything else they'd ever done.

Her husbands both had a bit of a dominant streak, one that reared its head with delightful frequency.

Her pussy and ass both clenched in anticipation, the erotic tension in the air heightening and sending a thrill of alarm through her.

"Yes. God, yes."

She rubbed against Clay, her body on fire. "You always do this to me. You make me so crazy that I can't even think."

Some of the tension drained from Clay's features. "Good. I don't want you to think. I just want you to feel. Feel how much we both love you." Bending, he touched his lips to hers while sliding a hand from her hips to her breast, closing his fingers over her nipple. "Want you. Need you."

Crying out, Jesse clung to him, shaken by the intensity of raw emotion and lust.

"I need you both so much. I was terrified that you'd found someone else, someone younger who could give you more children."

Clay groaned, brushing her jaw with his lips.

"You're everything to me, baby. I don't know how I ever lived without you. I know I can't ever do it again. I don't want any other woman. I don't care about more children. Between my son, Rio's, and yours, we have three, and they take enough of your time."

Lifting his head, he massaged her breast before rolling her nipple between his thumb and forefinger, his eyes flaring with heat when she cried out and bucked against him.

"I'm selfish. I want every minute I can have with you. I didn't know what happiness was until I met you. Damn it, Jesse. How could you not know? Christ, I have to have you. I swear, I could eat you alive."

Jesse sucked in a breath as he slid down her body, knowing just how decadent that mouth of his could be. Her body shook uncontrollably in anticipation of the pleasure to come. Her pulse tripped when Rio moved in closer and took her wrists in his, lifting them over her head.

Clay lowered his head to her slit, forcing yet another cry from her, each one seeming to spur them both to greater heights.

Clay's hands tightened on her thighs, holding them high and wide as he buried his face between them, sliding his tongue over her folds before concentrating on her clit. With slow strokes designed to drive her wild, he used his tongue on her clit—rapid flicks that made her jolt and cry out, the sensation as strong as if an electric current ran through her.

Rio grinned down at her, his eyes shining with the confidence of a man who knew how to pleasure his woman. "All spread out like a feast. Clay sure is enjoying that pussy."

He ran his hands over her, igniting flames everywhere he touched. His eyes gleamed with fascination, narrowing when she cried out and writhed beneath him.

"I've never in my life seen a woman more beautiful." Using a callused finger to circle her nipple, he held her hands in an iron grip, easily overcoming her struggles.

Jesse's cries got louder and more frantic as Clay sucked her clit into his mouth, the warning tingles of her impending orgasm becoming so strong she kicked at him in an involuntary struggle to escape. She wanted it badly, but the strength of it overwhelmed her.

So familiar, and yet always so exciting.

Rio squeezed her nipple lightly, applying just the right amount of pressure. "Come, darlin'. I love watching you try to hold back. You want to make it last, but this morning, you're not going to be able to."

The shock of Clay's teeth scraping lightly over her clit stunned her so much she froze, the tingling sensation exploding and racing from her clit outward. With a loud cry, she came, pressing down with her legs and arching as the rush of pleasure consumed her.

Releasing her thighs, Clay ran his hands over her abdomen and hips, using slow, light strokes of his tongue over her clit, keeping the waves of pleasure and shimmering heat rolling through her as he brought her down slowly.

She didn't have to open her eyes to know who touched her where. She knew the feel of their hands, the rhythm of their caresses as well as she knew her own name.

The familiarity hadn't lessened her need for either of them.

It only made it richer.

Clay and Rio *knew* her.

Her body

Her mind.

Her heart.

As Clay lifted his head, his eyes filled with hunger and satisfaction, she realized she knew them both just as well.

Even now, she could feel Clay's pride in the fact that's he'd made her come so easily. She could feel his anticipation, and the gleam in his narrowed gaze told her how much he'd enjoyed what he just did to her and how much he looked forward to more.

The hard edge of possessiveness in his eyes told her that he wanted to be the one in her ass, to cover her body with his in the bright morning light, and take her in the most dominant way possible for a man to take a woman.

Her puckered opening tingled with awareness and anticipation, making it difficult to breathe.

She could feel the love all around her, their seemingly endless fascination in her.

She also knew they hurt, and her shame in that had her reaching for both of them.

"I'm sorry. It's scary, isn't it?"

Clay lifted his head. "What is, baby?"

"Love. Real love. It's so strong. The thought of losing it scared me to death. It's so hard to believe sometimes."

Her body trembled, the small waves of heat still rippling through her. She let out a moan as Rio rolled to his back, taking her with him.

Settling her on top of him, Rio gathered her close, running his hands up and down her spine.

"Terrifying. You deserve to be spanked for what you put us through."

Lifting her hips, he lowered her again, impaling her on his cock with a groan, his hands firm on her hips to hold her steady.

"When I'm inside you, you're not thinking about anything else." He lifted her several inches, his eyes full of mischief and hunger as he lowered her again. "Fucking you seems to be the only way to keep you out of trouble."

Jesse's breath caught as he filled her again, making it difficult to speak. "That has to be—ah—the most—chau—damn, that feels good—chauvinistic and arrogant thing—oh, God—you've ever said."

Rio withdrew a bit and surged deep again. "Not by a long shot."

Moaning at the feel of every bump and ridge of his cock caressing her inner walls, Jesse moved into his thrusts, her desperate gulps of air growing louder.

"You're lucky you're both good at this."

When Clay moved in behind her, Rio thrust deep and pulled her down to his chest, his hands firm at her shoulders and back.

"We can handle *you*, darlin'. Easy, Jesse. Hold on tight while Clay gets inside you. Fuck. Hurry up, Clay. She's clenching on me the way she does when she wants us to hurry."

Clay groaned harshly and rubbed the cheeks of her ass, running his fingers down the crease and over her sensitive opening. "But she's not in charge here, now is she?"

Fisting her hands in the pillow below Rio's head, Jesse cried out, her pussy clenching on Rio's thick cock while her bottom hole tingled with anticipation.

"I will be soon. You're both suckers for me and you know it. Damn, I never get used to you taking me together."

Clay ran a hand over her back. "None of us do. It would be a pity, I think, if we ever did. I know how good it's going to feel to have my cock inside that tight ass, but each time is like the first time."

The tension in his voice spoke volumes about his level of excitement, an excitement that hadn't appeared to wane a bit in the last two years.

Clay's hands moved over her, sliding down to cup her bottom, making her quiver everywhere he touched her.

"You know, I think this is a perfect time to give you that spanking for scaring the hell out of us the way you did."

Jesse jolted, trying to lift off of Rio's chest, but Rio held firm.

"Clay! You can't be serious! You don't spank me anymore."

Leaning over her, Clay scraped his teeth over her shoulder.

"An oversight on our part—one that won't be repeated. We've obviously been too soft on you. You know damned well that what you did was foolish and could have gotten you hurt. Or worse. I can't go through something like that again, Jesse. You put us through hell. Did you really think you were going to get away with that?"

Jesse shuddered at the anger in Clay's voice. Alarmed now, Jesse struggled to get up, the realization that she'd somehow forgotten just how chauvinistic and dominant her men could be hitting her hard, and sending shivers of anticipation through her. She'd also forgotten what they were like in this mood—forceful and intense, and sometimes unpredictable.

"Clay, we need to talk about this." Apprehensive and aroused, she lifted slightly to look down into Rio's face, becoming even more nervous when she saw the determination and lingering fear in Rio's eyes.

Rio reached between them and pinched a nipple, his hard arm around her back like iron, and just as inflexible.

"The chance for talking was last night before you snuck out of here through the fucking bathroom window. Do you know how it felt to find you gone? Do you know how terrified we were?"

Clay slapped her ass, the sting setting off a riot of sensation from her ass to her clit and back again. "More terrified than you are now, that's for sure. If I had my way, Jesse Erickson, you wouldn't be able to sit down for a week."

He delivered another sharp slap to her other butt cheek, the heat from it mingling with the first slap and centering at her slit.

Clenching her teeth, she squeezed her eyes closed, wondering how she could have forgotten how much this excited her.

"You could have had car trouble."

Another slap. More heat.

Jesse wiggled, the warmth from the spanking making her pussy clench on Rio's cock, while at the same time intensifying the awareness of her puckered opening.

Her clit felt huge, the throbbing becoming even worse.

It always got to her, this position of vulnerability. They knew what it did to her, and that it pissed her off as much as it excited her.

"Stop spanking me, damn it. I swear when I get up, you're going to be sorry."

Hell, no wonder her sister always taunted Jake into spanking her.

Rio chuckled, groaning when she wiggled again. "Hell no, don't stop. She's fucking herself on my cock while you're heating that ass. Maybe she'll think before she ever does something like this to us again."

Clay delivered another slap. "I have no intention of stopping. If you'd had car trouble, you could have been stuck on a dark road out in the middle of nowhere."

Another slap, and then another, each earning cries from her—each creating more heat and building the awareness in her bottom hole. Wiggling her ass, she gasped when Clay slid a finger over her forbidden opening, stiffening when he chuckled.

He did it again, pressing lightly and making it sting.

"You want this ass filled and I'm not even done yet. I'm going to shove my cock in that tight ass and make it burn, like my guts burned last night when you almost got hurt in a hotel fire! What if we hadn't gotten to you? You. Could. Have. Been. Killed."

He punctuated each word with a slap on her ass, except the last. With a groan, he covered her back, his lips hot on her shoulder.

"My heart would have died with you."

Jesse arched as much as she could, allowing Rio better access to her breasts, the firm pinch of her nipples between his strong fingers sending arrows of tingling sizzles to her clit, ass, and pussy. Choking back a cry, she threw her head back. "I love you. Both. So much. Too much."

Her clit felt huge, throbbing to the beat of her heart, becoming so sensitive that each time she moved against Rio, it sent jolts of sizzling heat to her pussy and ass.

With no warning, a lubed finger was shoved into her ass, the shock of it stealing her breath.

"Never too much."

Clay sunk his teeth into her shoulder as he moved it inside her.

"Next time I won't be so nice."

Jesse squirmed on Rio, her ass clenching on the finger Clay slid deep inside her, clamping down on Rio's cock at the same time.

"Ah, God!" The feel of something invading her bottom never failed to shake her. It always felt too intimate, too naughty, and as with the spanking, made her feel vulnerable as hell, something her husbands used to their advantage.

Rio's hoarse curses mingled with her cries and whimpers, his groan rumbling beneath her, the vibrations of it racing over her heated skin.

"The way she clenches drives me crazy. Everything about her drives me crazy." He tugged a nipple, groaning when she cried out and clenched on him again. "*I* still owe her a spanking."

Clay slid his finger from her, igniting every nerve ending along the way. "I want to be there."

Jesse shivered at the threat, unable to catch her breath when Clay positioned the head of his cock against her puckered opening. As always, the vulnerability of her position filled her with trepidation, but the trust in her husbands made it possible to let herself go.

"Easy, baby. Hold on tight to Rio. My cock's going in there no matter how much you try to close against me." Clay's rough drawl sent a decadent thrill through her, telling her more than words just how much this excited him.

A shiver went up Jesse's spine as Clay pressed forward, a whimpered cry escaping when the head of his cock pushed through the tight ring of muscle and into her.

"Clay! Oh, God." She never got used to it—was never prepared for being so full, so taken.

Clay's hands firmed on her hips, his voice like shattered glass. "Rio, hold on to her."

Rio held her closer. "I've got her." Lifting his hips, he groaned. "Hurry up, damn it. She's gonna scream my name before we're through here."

"And mine." Clay forced his cock an inch deeper, withdrew slightly, and thrust again, pushing even deeper. "I'll bet she screams mine first."

Trembling helplessly, Jesse whimpered at the burning heat as Clay worked his cock into her, inch by incredible inch, forcing the delicate inner walls of her bottom to stretch to accommodate him.

Rio slid his hands lower, gripping her thighs to control her movements.

Clay held her hips with an equally firm grip. "Hell, I can never get over how tight her ass is."

Rio groaned, his eyes narrowed on hers as he thrust deep.

"Especially when we're both inside her."

Jesse threw her head back again, crying out as her husbands fucked her pussy and ass in a rhythm that drove her ruthlessly toward the edge. As Rio withdrew, Clay surged deep, only to withdraw until the head of his cock reached the tight ring of muscle while Rio thrust into her again.

Every thrust made her clench, making her feel even fuller. Her clit throbbed unbearably, so badly that she reached for it herself, only to have Rio slap her hand away.

"No way, darlin'. You've gotta pay."

Clay surged deep. "Never again."

Mini-explosions went off inside her, gathering to add to the tingling heat. "God! Clay!"

"Yes!" Gripping her waist, he withdrew several inches and surged deep again. "Mine."

Rio's face tightened, a mask of tortured concentration, groans of pleasure rumbling from his chest. Pinching her clit between his thumbs, he worked the swollen nub, setting her off.

Every nerve ending in her ass and pussy sizzled, her clit burning and pulsing beneath Rio's thumbs.

Sensation took over. She threw back her head, screaming Rio's name, her body stiffening as she clamped down on their cocks.

The waves engulfed her, rolling through her and tossing her everywhere. She couldn't hold on to anything, but knew they held her. She heard their groans as they came, felt the pulsing of the cocks inside her, but couldn't move.

Her voice became hoarse from screaming, but she had no idea what she said.

She only knew heat.

And the love all around her.

By slow increments, she became aware of Rio and Clay's crooning voices, the words of praise and love pouring over her. She became aware of the firm hands gentling on her body, caressing her and guiding her back down to earth.

After what could have been several minutes, or an hour, Jesse lifted her head from Rio's chest, smiling at the drowsy look in his eyes. "I love you so much it scares the hell out of me sometimes."

Rio grinned. "Back atcha, darlin'."

Clay placed a kiss on her back, rubbing her hip as he withdrew from her ass.

"Come on, baby. Let's get a shower."

Once in the shower, Clay backed her against the wall, his eyes fierce. "You're my life, Jesse. I couldn't live without you. The next time you get pissed at us—and you will—talk to us. Yell. Scream. Curse. Just don't run out. If you're scared, we face it together."

Lifting her face for his kiss, Jesse sighed. "Yes. I love you, Clay, more than I ever thought possible."

He gathered her against him, letting the warm water soothe the last of her tremors away. "You're my world, baby."

"And you're mine." She lifted her head, pushing back his wet hair. "No more lies. What did you mean about turning my world upside down?"

Clay frowned, staring down at her. "What do you mean—oh! Honey, it's not your world we were talking about. It was your sister's. Don't ask me anything else. Nat's going to be just fine."

Grinning, he began washing her. "You just worry about yourself. You're still in trouble, you know."

Pressing herself against him, she rubbed her breasts against his chest, adopting a look of innocence as she stared up at him through her lashes.

"Is there anything I can do to get out of trouble?"

A flash of heat shone in Clay's eyes before they narrowed. "Maybe. It's been a long time since you sat on my lap naked while we ate breakfast."

Happier than ever, Jesse pursed her lips, pretending to consider that. "Well, since the boys are away this weekend, I guess it would be all right."

Clay nodded once. "Good. Then afterward, I can spread you out on the table and have my dessert."

A cold burst of air made her shiver as Rio opened the shower door and stepped inside. With no warning, he wrapped an arm around her waist and pulled her against him, sliding a finger into her ass. "After that, I owe her a spanking."

Jesse gasped and went to her toes, holding on to Clay. "I have a feeling I won't be able to walk after this weekend."

Clay's hold firmed. "You sure as hell won't be able to run."

Working herself on Rio's finger, Jesse cupped Clay's cock. "Never again. I promise."

Clay covered her hand with his. "We're going to hold you to that, baby. You're stuck with us forever."

Jesse couldn't think of anything she treasured more than the love of her husbands. "Promise?"

"Promise. Now about that breakfast…"

Epilogue

With a combination of a moan and a sigh, Jesse leaned back against Rio. "I'm so glad we have these two days alone together."

She'd taken another shower, and afterward, had been too lethargic to even dry her hair before she joined Rio on the sofa. The feel of his fingers going through it had lulled her into a state halfway between sleep and wakefulness.

Sliding a hand under her thick robe, he caressed her thigh. "So am I. I think we need it." After a pause, he kissed her hair and cuddled her closer. "What's bothering you?"

She didn't know why it still surprised her when either Clay or Rio knew that something was wrong, but it always did. Turning her head, she brushed her lips over his strong jaw. "Do you ever regret that I can't have any more children?"

Rio stilled, looking at her in surprise. A few seconds later, he chuckled, topping her back over his arm and leaning over her. "Hell, is that what you've been worried about? The answer is no. Clay and I talked about it once, and to be honest, we were kind of glad you didn't seem to want to get the surgery to try. We didn't want to think about you going through an operation for one thing, but I remember those days. Sleepless nights and you'd be even more exhausted than you are now."

Running a hand over her belly, he grinned. "I told you, I'm selfish. I want every minute with you that I can get." With slow deliberation, he worked to untie her robe and spread it wide.

"Clay and I are very selfish when it comes to having time with you." His fingertips danced over her mound. "Would I risk having you mad at me again if I suggested that you hire a couple more people to work in the store?"

Jesse couldn't help but smile.

Her store had taken off far more than any of them had anticipated, especially once she'd gone online. It became increasingly difficult to keep up with orders, and as a result, she'd had to work late some nights when she would have rather been home with her husbands.

Looking up at him through her lashes, she spread her legs as the stirring at her slit made her needy for his attention there. "I'll let you try to talk me into it while we're riding tomorrow."

Rio grinned. "I'm sure I can manage to convince you. It's just as well that we didn't go out today. It's raining cats and dogs out there, and you need to rest today—not go out there and get sick."

Sucking in a breath as he lifted her and closed his mouth over her nipple, Jesse let her eyes flutter closed, consumed by the pleasure of Rio's touch. "I'm not fragile, Rio. I'd just rather spend a lazy day with both of you."

He used his tongue and teeth to tease her nipple, the sharp arrows of delight and need shooting straight to her slit. Both of her husbands had learned her body well, and knew just where and how to touch her to give the most pleasure, and turned her into a quivering mass of indescribable hunger.

"I'd rather get you wet right here."

Her clit throbbed incessantly, feeling swollen and achy, her inner thighs already coated with her juices.

She tried to relieve it by pressing her thighs together, but Rio anticipated her, keeping a hand between them to prevent it.

Chuckling, Rio lifted his head and brushed his lips over hers. "I know all your tricks, darlin'. Feeling a little needy, baby? It's just as well you planned to spend the day inside with us. You're going to be worn out after you get the spanking still coming to you."

Jesse shivered, trying to press her slit against his hand. Lifting a hand, she tangled it in his overlong hair to pull him closer, loving the feel of the silkiness against her fingers.

His kiss made her dizzy, as did the thought of Rio's brand of punishment.

Clay had always been more straightforward, but Rio had a devious side to him that she could never completely anticipate. He'd spanked her several times in the past, making each one a memorable occasion.

The idea of being spanked would have made her furious just a few years ago, but her husbands turned a spanking into an erotic adventure.

When Rio lifted his head, they were both breathing heavily. "When Clay gets back from Beau's store, you're going to get a surprise. Just thinking about it makes my cock hard as hell."

Jesse tried to laugh, but it erupted as a moan when Rio plunged a finger into her. "What kind of—oooh—surprise?" Dizzy, she lifted into his touch, moaning at the feel of his finger moving inside her.

Trailing the end of her plush robe over her nipple, Rio smiled down at her. "Instead of giving you the spanking you deserve, I have something a little more…intense in mind."

Arching into him, she struggled halfheartedly when he tied her wrists together, her heart pounding with anticipation. "You know that I'll get even with you for whatever mean thing you have planned."

It was a threat she used on them all the time, one that gave all of them a great deal of enjoyment. With her husbands, she'd learned how to play, and never tired of it.

Rio's devious laugh danced over her skin like hundreds of erotic fingers. "That's part of the fun. Then, I can get back at you for what you did to me, and so on, and so on…Christ, woman, I love you."

Her vision blurred, tears filling her eyes as love for him swelled inside her. "I love you, too, Rio. So much." Lifting her bound hands over his head to circle his neck, she pulled him closer. "I can't even imagine life without you now. I think that's what hit me so hard last night. I need you and Clay too much. It scares me sometimes."

Rio smiled slowly, a smile filled with love and tenderness. "And we need you." Withdrawing his finger from her pussy, he teased her folds. "We couldn't live without you, Jesse. You're too important to us. The thought of you getting hurt scares the hell out of us."

"Which is why she got a red ass."

Jesse jolted at the deep rumble of Clay's voice coming from the doorway. Tilting her head back, she watched him approach, smiling when he bent to touch his lips to hers in an upside down kiss.

Rio slowly withdrew his finger and surged to his feet. "Give it to me."

Clay grinned, wrapping his arms around Jesse, his eyes full of the love she'd come to depend on. "Give *her* to me."

Jesse found herself being transferred from Rio's arms to Clay's, her wrists, still tied together with the belt, wrapped around Clay's neck.

Dropping to the sofa with her in his arms, Clay pushed the edges of her robe apart and ran his hands over her. "Jesse, I swear, if you ever pull a stunt like the one you pulled last night, I'm going to tie you to the bed and keep you there."

His voice held a hard edge of remembered fear as he gathered her close and buried his face against her neck. "Please don't ever scare us like that again. I can't believe you would think we would ever want another woman. Apparently, I haven't done a good enough job of showing you what you mean to me."

Hugging him to her, Jesse blinked back tears. "Oh, Clay. You have. It was just me. I love you and Rio so much it scares me."

Clay lifted his head and stared down at her. "Sometimes, when I look at you, I can't breathe." He ran his hand over her hair, his eyes dark with emotion. "I look at you and I think, *this incredible woman is mine.* I hold you at night and listen to you breathe, and thank God that you came into my life."

Rio knelt on the sofa between her knees, pushing them apart. "Enough mush. Our wife needs a firmer hand. Maybe then she'll remember not to do something so dangerous again."

She knew her husbands well, and like the other men who lived in Desire, they felt compelled to discipline their wife in the hope of keeping her from danger.

The punishment they doled out usually provided pleasure so intense that it bordered on pain, and wasn't punishment at all.

The women who lived in Desire understood why the men did it.

They did it for their own peace of mind and their own need to be in control.

The women enjoyed their punishments, and Jesse had a sneaky suspicion that the men knew it, but no one spoke about it. All the women she knew put up a token protest, which appeased the men, and everyone got what they wanted.

Confident that one word from her would put a stop to their high-handedness, Jesse arched her bare mound toward Rio, her clit already throbbing in anticipation.

Shivering as Clay ran his hands over her breasts, she glanced at Rio, her stomach tightening when he produced a small whip. "What are you planning to do to me?"

They'd spanked her several times in the last couple of years, something she fought but that ultimately gave all three of them a great deal of pleasure, but the small whip that Rio held now was something new.

Rio grinned, his eyes dancing with devious intent. "Clay gave you a spanking, but my brand of punishment is a little more intense."

Unwrapping her arms from around his neck, Clay sat back, holding her arms above her head with one hand, while dancing the fingers of the other over her breasts. "Looks like you're in trouble, baby."

The tug to her nipple sent a current of electricity to her clit and had her arching against him, but she couldn't take her eyes from the whip. Sucking in a breath as Rio lowered it to her mound, Jesse began to tremble, her pussy clenching at the feel of the small leather tip moving over her bare skin.

"Rio!"

"Yes, darlin'?"

"I swear, if you hurt me—"

His wicked smile sent a thrill through her, one that made her stomach clench and her clit throb so hard she couldn't stop writhing.

Clay's hand slid down her body, pausing to dance over her abdomen before moving lower to part her folds. "When have either one of us ever hurt you? Now, accept your punishment like a good girl."

Jesse glanced at Clay, not taking her eyes from Rio for more than a second or two. "You're awfully brave right now, but I'm not going to be in this position forever." She thought of all the things she could do to retaliate, knowing that each one she imagined would bring all three of them a great deal of pleasure.

Clay laughed softly, a sound that was like music to her ears. "If you get too sassy, I'll just tie you to the bed and fuck that tight ass again."

She shivered, crying out when Rio ran the leather tip of the whip over her clit. Her bottom clenched in remembered pleasure, and if she knew her husbands at all, a pleasure that would be coming again very soon.

Clay groaned, running a hand over her belly as he stared down at her. "I swear, those sounds you make when you're aroused make me crazy to have you. Hell, I'm always crazy to have you, and for you to run away, thinking I could want anyone else, pisses me off." He slid his hand lower, parting her folds again, his eyes steady on hers as Rio raised the whip and brought it down on her clit.

Crying out in shock, Jesse struggled against Clay, trying to yank her hands from his hold, desperate to protect her clit. Seconds later, the sting hit her, followed by a sizzling heat that had her whimpering and fighting her husbands to close her legs against more.

It was so hot, it burned, the sizzling sensation so much like an orgasm, she didn't know if she was coming or not.

Screaming Clay's name, she threw herself at him. "Clay, I can't stand it. Oh, my God. It won't stop stinging."

"No more." Clay's deep baritone rang out as he gathered her closer. "She's too delicate, Rio."

"Kiss my ass. I'm not delicate." She couldn't stop rocking her hips, the fluttering inside her tantalizing her into wanting more. She'd been down this path several times, and yet each time proved to be as exciting and surprising as the last.

Her love and hunger for them never waned.

Instead, the familiarity made it stronger.

Rio chuckled, that low, deep sound that never failed to make Jesse's heart race. "She's fine." He pressed a firm finger into her pussy, thrusting several times before withdrawing. "Better than fine. She's soaking wet, and her pussy's clampin' down like she's hungry. You hungry to be fucked, darlin'."

Jesse's struggles proved useless, and with Clay leaning over her, she couldn't see Rio at all, but she heard the amusement and sexual tension in his voice. "Bastard! Stop teasing me."

As the sizzling sensation spread, Jesse kicked at him, doubling her efforts when he laughed and ran a finger over her throbbing clit, before bringing the whip down on it again, this time even lighter than before.

He ran his lips over her inner thigh, stopping short of her slit. "What's the matter, darlin'? That clit giving you trouble?"

"Fuck you!" Struggling harder, and disconcerted because she couldn't see him or anticipate him, Jesse kicked at him while struggling to get free of Clay's grip.

Her clit burned, her pussy clenched repeatedly, and the tingling even spread to tease her puckered opening.

Her husbands, at six and a half feet tall and packed with hard muscle they'd earned working on the ranch, overcame her struggles with an ease that she'd come to know well.

Their familiar touch so arousing and so familiar that she could tell their caresses apart even in the dark.

Her husbands' strength had been both a source of frustration and one of incredible delight to her, and both came into play now.

Clay grinned down at her, his eyes playful, but watchful as they always were when he and Rio played this way. "Looks like Rio's got you all worked up with that whip. I guess we're going to have to use it more often." He hooked an arm beneath her knees and brought them close to her chest, exposing her clit, pussy, and ass completely, and leaving her defenseless to protect herself against Rio's wicked brand of punishment.

Her clit felt huge, the warning tingles she'd become so used to since Clay and Rio came into her life making it pulse in time to her own heartbeat. Her pussy clenched repeatedly, clamping down on the finger Rio slid inside her, her hips bucking as he slid another finger into her.

He teased her, pressing against the spot inside her that made her crazy with need, only to withdraw again. "Not yet, darlin'."

She'd been so close, only to be yanked from the edge, leaving her clenching at emptiness and crying out with frustration.

The silence that followed, filled with sexual tension, lengthened until Jesse couldn't stand it anymore. She couldn't hold back her whimpers, her breathing ragged as she waited for Rio to use the whip again. "Do it, damn you."

She sucked in a breath, and then another, the anticipation driving her insane.

Clay held her in place, his hold firm and inescapable as he stared down at her, his eyes gleaming with heat and adoration, a look she'd never been able to resist. "You like that. I'm going to have to go back to Beau's store and buy some more toys."

His slow, delicate brand of loving always thrilled her, his need to give her what she needed before she even realized what she needed had been a constant source of delight to her.

Rio, on the other hand, teased her mercilessly, dragging out foreplay until she became so desperate, she'd do anything to come.

Sliding a finger into her, Rio fucked her pussy with slow strokes before withdrawing again.

Each time he withdrew, she held her breath in expectation, her entire body shaking as she waited for him to strike her clit again. Instead, he chuckled and pressed his finger into her again, teasing her until she bucked in Clay's arms before withdrawing again.

The second time he did it, she started cursing at him, and by the third, she wanted to hit him.

Fighting got her nowhere, but she couldn't resist struggling, crying out in alarm when Rio began to run the tip of the whip up and down her slit. Since she couldn't see him, she settled for glaring at Clay, holding him equally responsible for her predicament. "You gonna fuck me, Rio, or are you going to play with your toys all day?"

Rio laughed out loud, and even without seeing him, she knew his beautiful eyes would be twinkling with mischief and gleaming with heat. "You are my toy, darlin'. Now, be still so I can have a taste. I don't want you to come until we're both inside you."

"I'm going to kill you the first chance I get. Oh, God." Jesse couldn't hold back a moan, one that made both Clay and Rio laugh softly.

Rio's tongue moved over her folds, the hot, velvety feel of it sending her senses soaring, the threat of it touching her tingling clit filling her with bubbling anticipation.

It felt so good, so intimate.

The heat spread, nearly consuming her. She needed to come. Badly.

So close.

They'd played this game often, and it was a game they all loved.

Clay and Rio would do their best to keep her on the edge and not let her go over. Usually they won, but the times that she'd come and they'd started all over again made fighting to come irresistible.

Crying out when Rio's tongue slid over her clit, she wiggled her hips to get the touch she wanted, but Rio merely laughed again, slapped her bottom, and straightened. "Nice try, darlin'."

Rubbing her legs when Clay released them, he smiled down at her. "You're too close, and I want to be inside that tight ass when you come."

Clay lifted her, swinging her to straddle him. "You can't blame her for trying. Sometimes we let her win." Lifting her to her knees, he made quick work of shoving his jeans down before lowering her again. "Not this time, though. After seeing her take that whip, I want her too much and can't wait."

Jesse's breath rushed out in a low moan of bliss when he lowered her onto his cock, always startled at the feel of his cock filling her. Fisting her hands in the soft cotton shirt covering his shoulders, she used her knees to move on him, crying out at the friction on her too sensitized clit.

"I can't, oh, that feels good, believe you would say that." Conscious that behind her, Rio stripped out of his clothes and started rolling on a condom, Jesse kept trying to turn to get a glimpse of him, not willing to miss any chance of seeing either one of her gorgeous husbands naked.

Sliding his big hands to her waist, Clay somehow managed to stroke her skin and hold her in place at the same time, his rough calluses sending shivers through her. "Say what, baby?"

Moaning at the feel of Rio moving in behind her, she threw her head back and clenched on Clay's cock, thrilling at his groan. "You said that whipping me excited you. Hurting me excites you?"

Clay pulled her close, his grip like iron. "Never. I would cut off my own hands before I hurt you." He kissed her, a hard kiss filled with emotion and desperation, one that left her breathless. His eyes searched hers as if he wanted to make sure she believed him. "I only want you to be happy, baby. I only want you to feel good. I wouldn't hurt a hair on your head and you know it."

Leaning her back over his arm, he slid his hand down her abdomen, making her stomach muscles quiver. He leaned over her, his eyes hooded and dark. "Tell me this doesn't feel incredible."

Jesse cried out at the stroke of his thumb over her clit, sucking in a breath when Rio bent to kiss a nipple. Her clit burned, warning her that she was about to go over, and with a cry, she rocked her hips to get the friction she needed.

"Oh, God! Yes." His callused thumb against her clit felt like heaven.

Every light stroke sent her higher, the slow caress of his thumb over her clit holding her spellbound. She slowed, whimpering at the astonishing sensation as the pleasure slowly built. "So good. So good."

Clay groaned and removed his finger, grabbing her wrists when she started to fight him.

"No. No. Damn it, I was so close. Clay, Please!" The need to come, like a living, breathing thing, clawed at her. With a cry of frustration, she yanked her hands from his hold and pulled at his shirt. "You son of a bitch!"

Clay smiled and wrapped his arms around her, pulling her to his chest, easily overcoming her struggles. "Poor baby. Admit it. That clit is so sensitive now that the slightest touch makes you wild."

Rio moved in behind her, sliding his hands around her to cup her breasts, his thumbs moving with a slow, firm pressure that he knew she loved. "Admit it, darlin'. You like the whip."

Jesse knew how devious they could be, and she knew they'd torture her with pleasure until she admitted it. "Yes, damn it. Now, fuck me."

Rio released her with a laugh. "With pleasure."

Pressed against Clay's chest, Jesse gripped his shoulders and tried not to stiffen.

She knew what was coming, and knew that once they were inside her, she would be helpless to do anything except hold on for the ride.

Even knowing they wouldn't hurt her, and knowing that all three of them would get a great deal of pleasure, she could never quite fight her initial panic, a fact they both seemed to realize, because they always comforted her as they took her.

Clay rubbed his hands up and down her back. "Easy, baby. Rio's gonna go nice and slow. You know that. You know how good it's gonna feel."

Gripping Clay tighter, Jesse stiffened when Rio pressed his lubed finger into her bottom, the initial shock of helplessness forcing a cry from her.

The change in their breathing thrilled her, the harsh sounds of tension so familiar and exciting.

Each time she moved, groans and low curses poured from them, deep and filled with hunger. The sexual tension vibrating from them couldn't be mistaken, their touch becoming more demanding by the minute.

Expecting Rio's usual playfulness, Jesse jolted when he yanked her hair aside and scraped his teeth over her shoulder.

With a groan, he pressed the head of his cock against her puckered opening. "Christ, woman. How the hell could you ever think we didn't want you?"

Her bottom hole burned at the pressure as his cock pressed insistently against the tight ring of muscle, forcing it to give way.

A cry escaped as he pressed his cock into her, the hand he pressed against her back not allowing her to move. Curling her toes, she held on to Clay as Rio paused with the head of his cock just inside her.

"I can't wait." Rio's deep growl signified a lack of control she seldom saw in him. "I want her too fucking much." His hands tightened on her hips as he growled again, his hips thrusting forward and filling her with more of his cock.

Whimpering at the full, stretched feeling, she buried her face against Clay's chest. "Oh, God. So full. Oh, God, it burns. I want more."

With one hand low on her back, and the other at the back of her head, Clay held her close. "It's amazing, isn't it? It's even stronger than when we first took you, stronger than when we first married."

Jesse blinked back tears, once again overwhelmed by the love she felt for Clay and Rio. "Every day. I love you both more every day. Too much. I can never get enough. Oh, God. Move. I can't stand it."

She'd never expected to love again, never knew love could be so powerful—or need could be so all-consuming.

When Clay gripped her waist, and Rio gripped her hips, Jesse sucked in a breath, staring into Clay's out as her breath erupted as a cry of hunger.

Their moves had become so familiar, and she knew that both of them were about to move. She wanted it. She needed it.

Still, a flare of panic had her stiffening.

Rio groaned, lifting her a little more off of Clay's chest. "We all know what's coming, don't we?"

"God, yes!" Jesse couldn't hold back a whimper as they moved, quickly establishing a rhythm that left her reeling. She'd never in her life experienced anything like Clay and Rio's lovemaking, and when they took her at the same time, filling her completely, it was nothing short of astounding.

The hands at her waist tightened as Clay lifted her and withdrew until just the head of his cock remained inside her, while Rio tightened his grip on her hips and surged deep into her ass.

They moved slowly at first, their cocks creating a delicious friction against her inner walls. As one cock surged into her, the other withdrew in a mind-numbing rhythm that kept a cock continuously thrusting into her.

The thrust of a cock filling her pussy, followed by the surge of a cock into her ass. Over and over and over until the sensations from both blended together into something that went far beyond sex.

She clung to Clay, while both Clay and Rio clung to her, every nuance of their lovemaking felt by all three of them, something they'd all come to cherish very much.

The sounds of her husbands' groans and low curses blended with her cries, filling the room with the tortured sounds of their lovemaking.

Their cocks felt so hard, like steel moving inside her, so thick that she could feel every bump and ridge as they took her.

So hard. So hot. So breathtaking.

Clay growled, a deep sound that rumbled in his chest, vibrating against her breasts. "Jesus, Jesse. Fuck. So fucking tight."

Rio's hands tightened. "Yes. Ah, God, Jesse. Christ, there's nothing better than being inside you. She okay?"

Clay clenched his jaw, his face tight with same sexual tension she heard in Rio's voice. Sliding his hands up her sides, he ran his thumbs over her breasts. "She's better than okay. She's perfect. So hot. Silky heat."

Shaking uncontrollably, Jesse threw her head back, her breath catching when Clay slid his hands down to her thighs. Moaning at his gentle massage, she jolted, crying out when he ran his thumbs over her clit, making it tingle even hotter.

She bucked to get away, to get more, the sensation so strong, she let out a long wail of ecstasy.

Her own movements worked her harder and faster on both cocks, taking them deeper than before.

Clay and Rio reacted immediately, cursing as they adjusted their grips on her, holding her still, but she'd already passed the point of no return.

A fine sheen of perspiration covered her body as the tingling spread, consuming her. It erupted in her clit, and in a shower of sparks, touched her everywhere.

Her husbands groaned, cursing inventively, and started thrusting again.

Currents of sizzling heat raced over her, and with a hoarse cry, she came, her pussy and ass clenching on the cocks filling her.

Their cocks, thick and impossibly hard, seemed to lengthen and thicken inside her, making the sensation of being filled even more intense.

The waves of current continued to wash over her, her body jolting in their arms. Her mind went blank, the pleasure still rolling through her

With low groans of completion, they came inside her, their cocks pulsing inside her pussy and ass as they surged deep into her.

With a whimper, she slumped against Clay, gulping in air in an effort to catch her breath.

Rio shuddered behind her. "I think we're gonna have to reserve that whip for special occasions."

Wrapping an arm around her from behind, Rio buried his face in her hair and began to slowly withdraw from her, holding her closely when she shivered as the head of his cock slid past the tight ring of muscle. "It almost killed me."

Dropping his head to rest on the back of the sofa, Clay chuckled, a sound of relaxed satisfaction. "Yeah, but I don't think it has anything to do with the whip. I think it's the woman we were both smart enough to marry."

Cupping her breasts, he massaged gently, his gaze watchful and indulgent. "You okay, baby?"

Leaning back against Rio, Jesse reached up to rub Clay's forearms, feeling warm, loved, and cherished. "I'm great, especially if I don't have to move for the next couple of hours."

With a smile, Clay gathered her close, tucking her head under his chin. "I could stay like this all day."

Rio tucked her robe around her. "How the hell did you lose your socks?"

Jesse smiled against Clay's chest as Rio slid them back on her. "You both take such good care of me." Pushing against Clay's chest, she straightened, looking back and forth between them.

"I've never been treated like this. I've never been loved this way."

Aware of their sharpened interest, Jesse shrugged. "I know. I think into things too much. Usually I just spend all day happy and feel like the luckiest woman in the world."

Blowing out a breath, she shook her head, lifting her gaze to Clay's. "Sometimes I just look at the two of you and can't believe it's real. It's like a dream, and I'm afraid I'm going to wake up and find that it's all gone."

Clay's eyes narrowed. "And when you walked in and heard our conversation, the dream turned into a nightmare?"

"Yeah." Remembering the way she'd felt at that moment, Jesse shuddered, her stomach clenching.

Clay lifted her chin, staring into her eyes. "I'll love you until the day I die, Jesse Erickson. Never forget that."

From behind, Rio hugged her. "You've ruined us for anyone else, darlin'. I can't even imagine a life without you in it. I love you, Jesse. And if you ever forget, I'll just have to remind you."

Blinking back tears, Jesse smiled. "Just promise me that when I get scared, you won't let me go."

Clay grinned. "That's a promise, baby."

Rio knelt beside her, bending to touch his lips to hers. "You're never getting away from us."

Wrapped in the heat of their bodies, Jesse nodded and slumped against Clay. Relaxed and replete, she let her eyes close and listened to their breathing and soft murmurs of love.

And vowed to herself to put her insecurities aside and live the dream they'd created together—a dream she'd never thought possible.

THE END

WWW.LEAHBROOKE.NET

SIREN
Publishing

BLADE'S DESIRE: ADORING KELLY

MORE DESIRE, OKLAHOMA 2

The Leah Brooke Collection

Everlasting Classic

BLADE'S DESIRE: ADORING KELLY

More Desire, Oklahoma 2

LEAH BROOKE
Copyright © 2014

Chapter One

Kelly Royal watched her tall, dark, and incredibly handsome husband as he got ready to go to work, once again mesmerized by the sheer strength and sexuality surrounding him.

The power and grace in his lean, muscular frame never failed to make her heart beat faster, creating a yearning inside her that never waned.

She wondered if she'd ever get used to the fact that such an incredible man loved her.

Leaning back against the large, heavy dresser, she let her gaze move over him as she had hundreds of times before, still a little dazed each time he looked at her with eyes shining with love or dark with concern.

He was everything to her, and he made it clear, by word and by deed, that she was the most important thing in the world to him.

It still amazed her.

He'd pulled his hair back, as he always did before going to the club, in a style that suited him and emphasized his sharp, chiseled features.

With his high cheekbones, glittering black eyes, dark skin of his ancestors, and hair as black as midnight, he looked every inch a warrior.

Her warrior.

He fought her demons—her fears and insecurities—with a fierceness and single-mindedness that didn't allow for failure.

He was her rock.

After suffering two miscarriages, the news that she'd become pregnant again had both thrilled and terrified her, and she knew it had the same effect on him.

Blade tried not to let his fear show, and had been a pillar of strength through her pregnancy, but he watched her like a hawk and treated her with kid gloves.

She'd learned to read her husband's moods—a necessary skill for a submissive when dealing with her Master—and knew just how scared he was, for her, and for the baby.

It shone in his eyes at times before he could mask it. She felt it in his touch, a desperation he couldn't quite hide.

He teased her out of her grumpy moods, rocked her and rubbed her swollen abdomen when the baby wouldn't settle, and fussed over her almost constantly to eat and to rest.

Nothing escaped his notice.

He hadn't slept through the night in months.

She'd waken several times to find him watching her. She'd witnessed the horror in his eyes when she'd woken from a sound sleep several weeks ago, gasping for air.

Blade had been like a wild man, hovering over her and lifting her swollen body with an ease that never failed to astound her. Even though she'd been able to catch her breath, he'd bundled her in blankets and raced with her to the doctor's office, murmuring softly to her the entire time.

The hell in his eyes had been unimaginable.

The doctor had assured them that it had only been the weight of the baby pressing on her lungs, but Blade had been scared to death of letting her fall asleep without him nearby ever since.

Since then, he'd slept sitting up, propped with pillows, with her in his arms. Night after night, he held her while she slept, barely getting any sleep himself, and every movement she made brought him awake in an instant.

His attentiveness and protectiveness, so much a part of him, became even more pronounced.

She couldn't have asked for anything more in a husband.

Still, she couldn't help worrying about him, and knew that things between them had changed. Altered.

He'd always been everything to her, and given her everything she'd ever needed or wanted.

But, he looked at her differently now, and she didn't know if she'd ever be what he needed again.

And it scared the hell out of her.

She could never fully explain to him how much his strength and love had gotten her through her miscarriages and this pregnancy, and she wanted to show him. She needed to give to him as much as he'd given to her.

"Kelly?"

Blinking, she lifted her gaze to his, giving him the reassuring smile that had become automatic.

"Yes. Sorry, my mind wandered. It usually does when I look at you."

He crossed the room to her, his graceful strides making her heart beat faster. "Nice try." Taking her hands in his, he lifted them to his lips, his eyes dark with concern. "Something's wrong. What is it?"

She loved him so much, it weakened her knees. She'd been such a burden to him for so long, and hated that he worried so much for her. She hated the stress she caused him, and hated that he never laughed anymore. "I'm fine, Blade. Stop fussing."

Blade frowned, clearly not believing her. Moving in behind her, he held her close, running his hands over her swollen abdomen in a loving gesture she'd come to adore. "I like fussing over you. Something's bothering you. What is it?" He spoke in the same soft tone he'd used ever since her first miscarriage, as if afraid of scaring her.

When she'd first met him, she'd been terrified of him and the way he'd made her feel. Her ex-boyfriend had been abusive in every way, and getting involved with a man as masculine as Blade, a man who didn't even attempt to hide the fact that he liked to dominate women, scared her to death.

He'd been patient and loving with her, and she'd eventually come to trust him completely.

She'd learned trust at his hands. Learned to love with his guidance.

She'd learned that sex could bring pleasure, and Blade had given her more than she'd ever thought possible. She'd given herself to him completely. In every way.

In doing so, they'd established a bond so strong and secure that she'd felt almost as if she were a part of him, and he of her.

It was a connection she didn't want to lose.

Placing her hands over his, she leaned back against him, grateful for his support. "You worry about me all the time. I hate being such a burden to you."

"Is my son kicking you again, baby?" He rocked her in his arms, another habit he'd acquired during her first pregnancy.

She couldn't help but smile at his tone, a deep silky tone that, with the slightest change in inflection, could comfort, arouse, or send a chill of apprehension through her.

Kelly couldn't help but smile at Blade's conviction that she carried a boy, even though they'd told the doctor that they didn't want to know the baby's sex. "Yes, but he's not as energetic as he was earlier." Tired and irritable, she just wanted to lie in bed and watch television, but knew that if she went to bed in front of him, he would just worry even more. Wanting to change the subject, she turned her head, looking up at him over her shoulder.

"You look very sexy tonight. Of course, you always look sexy, but when you dress for the club…"

She didn't want to think about the women that would be there. Scantily clad, if they wore anything at all, and probably all stunningly beautiful. Thin.

"Hmm." Blade nuzzled her neck in a particularly sensitive spot that he'd mastered long ago. "It's nice to know my beautiful wife thinks I'm sexy, especially since I think she's the sexiest, most desirable woman on earth."

Turning away, she blinked back tears, angry that he would never see her as sexy again, scared that he wouldn't be able to find the pleasure in her he had before. "Don't patronize me, Blade. I'm fat and I waddle."

She tried to push him away, but he cuddled her closer. "Let go of me."

God, she wanted him so much.

It was a need that would go unsatisfied. Blade had stopped making love to her months earlier, too scared of hurting her and causing another miscarriage.

"Never." Sliding his hands higher, he began to massage her breasts, his touch soothing on her aching body. "You're mine forever. I'll never let you go. Still sensitive, baby?"

Moaning at the pleasure, she slumped against him, the heat of his body against hers easing her aching body. "Hmm." Turning her head, she lifted her face to his. "Yes, but don't stop. I ache everywhere. I'm so fat that I can't even get out of a chair without help. Very sexy, huh?"

Wincing at the tightening around her abdomen, she stiffened. Not wanting to worry him, she bit back a moan, grateful when it passed almost immediately. "You've spent months handling me with kid gloves. I was scared of you when we met, even though I was attracted to you—had feelings for you. You were so patient with me, until I could let go, and be what you needed." Smiling she closed her eyes. "What we both needed."

Opening her eyes again, she sighed. "But ever since I got pregnant the first time, it seems all you've been doing is taking care of me. Handling me as if I'll break. I'm sure this isn't what you expected when you married me."

Blade rubbed her abdomen, his lips warm against her ear. "I got even more than I could have ever hoped for."

Turning her in his arms, he frowned down at her, his eyes full of concern. "Kelly, you're my life. You know how much I love you, don't you?"

Love for him swelled inside her. Reaching up, she flattened her hands on his chest, flexing her fingers into the hard muscle she knew so well. "Blade, you've been so wonderful through my pregnancies and miscarriages. You've been my rock."

Blinking back tears, she clenched her jaw when another pain hit her—like a rubber band tightening around her abdomen. "I don't know what I would have done without you."

"You'll never have to be without me, baby."

Scared now, she looked up at him through her lashes, and voiced the fear that had been choking her for months. "We're never going to be the same, are we?"

Blade stilled, his eyes narrowing. "Kelly, what the hell are you talking about?" Wrapping an arm around her, he led her to the bed, urging her to sit. "You're tired, honey, and you're in pain."

Wincing at the ache in her back, she laid on her side, curling her body as she searched for a comfortable position. "I know you love me, Blade. I know how much you want this baby. I'm just afraid. You haven't touched me in months. I see the way you look at me. Something's missing. I miss that look."

Blade positioned himself to lean over her protectively. "Of course I want this baby. I want you, too, Kelly. I've never stopped wanting you."

Blowing out a breath, he laid a hand on her abdomen as he knelt on the floor beside her. His expression softened, but his eyes narrowed in concern. "You're tired, baby, and uncomfortable. Just stay here. I'll call the club and tell them—"

She didn't want him to see her this way. She hated the fear in his eyes. Knowing he needed a break from all the tension, she forced a smile. "No. Just go. I'll be fine. I feel better already. I'll just lie here for a while."

Leaning close, Blade cupped her jaw, brushing his lips over hers. "I always want you, Kelly, but we both have to be patient. You really don't expect me to spank your gorgeous ass while you're pregnant, do you? Or put clamps on already tender nipples?"

Kelly swallowed the lump in her throat. It had been so long since he'd done either of those things. "Blade, you love sex. Love to play, but you haven't touched me in months. Even after I have the baby, it'll be a while before I recover. Then, I'll be nursing. You're never going to want me that way again. You're too scared of hurting me now. I see it in your eyes."

A sob escaped before she could prevent it. "Love isn't going to be enough for us, is it? I'm going to lose you."

"Kelly, that's enough." The impatience in his tone scared her.

She'd never known Blade to be impatient about anything.

Cursing, he ran his hand over her abdomen again. Closing his eyes, he blew out a breath, before opening them again, holding her gaze with his tortured one. "You're getting all worked up over nothing." Frowning, he glanced at her stomach before meeting her gaze again. "You're having contractions, aren't you? You're in even more pain than I thought. Were you even going to tell me?"

He shot to his feet, cursing soundly. "We'll deal with that later. Stay here. I'm going to go call your doctor."

Kelly winced, her entire body tightening as another contraction hit her. Overcome with pain and fear, she reached for her husband. "Blade, it's too soon. The baby's not due for another month."

He smiled, his eyes gentling, but still swirling with fear. "I know, baby. Everything'll be fine."

Relying on his strength, she gripped his hand while he used the other to hold his cell phone to his ear. Listening to his short, terse conversation with her doctor, she closed her eyes and sought a more comfortable position. The sudden rush of warmth startled her. "Oh, God. Blade, my water broke."

Please, God, don't let us lose another baby.

Blade turned away, whispering frantically into the phone before turning back to her. His eyes held a hint of wildness when they met hers again, but his tone remained calm and controlled. "Calm down, baby. An ambulance is coming to take us to the hospital."

She gripped his hand and tried to sit up, but found herself lowered to her back. "No! No ambulance. You drive me." The thought of having to ride in an ambulance again terrified her.

"I'm losing the baby, aren't I? This can't be happening again!"

Blade gathered her in his arms, lifting her against his hard chest. Sitting on the edge of the bed, he settled her on his lap, wrapping her in a blanket. "Calm down, baby. Please. Breathe slowly. In and out. That's my girl."

"Blade, it's too early. The lungs aren't ready, but my water already broke. The baby's coming. He's not moving." Terrified, and in agony, she held on to him, looking into his eyes.

Looking to him for guidance and support.

Her rock.

As her husband, her lover, her Master, she'd learned to rely on his guidance and strength, never more so than at that moment.

Blade's tense smile didn't reach his eyes, his playful tone an obvious effort to reassure her. "I'm glad you finally realize I'm right and we're having a boy. Now, just relax and take nice, slow breaths for me."

"Why do we have to go by ambulance? Why can't you drive me? Something's wrong, isn't it?" She couldn't calm down, and struggled to slow her breathing, but the panic and fear nearly choked her.

"Of course not." Rocking her, he buried his face in her hair. "Everything's going to be just fine. We're going to the hospital and having a baby. Eight months, Kelly. The baby'll be just fine, and so will you."

"Then why do we have to go by ambulance?"

* * * *

Blade forced a smile to hide his horror. "Because I want to hold you, and it'll be faster." Every minute seemed to last an eternity. Murmuring to Kelly, he tried to keep the terror out of his voice as he waited, while at the same time holding her gaze.

He knew what he had to do to calm her, but it had never been as difficult as now.

He'd wrapped her in the blanket, hoping she didn't see the blood, but could even now feel it soaking the front of his trousers.

She looked pale—too pale. Her eyes glimmered with pain and fear, her hand moving almost continuously over her swollen abdomen.

God, he loved her. If anything happened to her…

The sound of the siren piercing the night sky had to be the most wonderful sound he'd ever heard.

She was too damned pale!

Her grip on him didn't seem as strong as before, her small, pale hands almost lifeless in his. The fear and love in her eyes ripped at his heart, the trust in them giving him the strength he needed to push back the mind-numbing terror.

Forcing a smile, he touched his lips to hers, tightening his hold as if that would keep her from slipping away. "The ambulance is here. Just calm down. The doctor's going to meet us at the hospital, and everything's going to be fine, baby."

Lifting her as gently as possible, he fought the urge to run outside, knowing that scaring her would only make things worse. As he'd expected, the ambulance attendants rushed toward him, along with Rafe Delgatto, one of the town deputies in Desire.

Rafe stopped abruptly, his eyes widening in horror when he saw the blanket wrapped around Kelly. Before he could say anything, Blade shook his head in a barely perceptible movement, glancing meaningfully to where Kelly rested her head against his shoulder with her eyes closed.

Rafe nodded, his expression softening when Kelly turned toward him. "I heard the call on the radio and rushed right over." He touched Kelly's arm, smiling when she lifted her head. "Hi, honey. Looks like you're ready to have this baby. You feeling okay?"

Shaking, Kelly lifted her head and gave Rafe a tremulous smile. "I'm fine. My water broke, so I guess this is it."

Rafe inclined his head, walking with them toward the waiting stretcher. "I think I'll follow you in. There'll be a lot of excitement in town when everyone finds out."

Blade lowered his wife to the stretcher, smiling to hide his fear. "Let's go have a baby."

As the paramedics lifted her into the ambulance and began taking her vital signs, Blade turned his head, never taking his eyes from his beloved wife. "Rafe, can you give Jesse a call? Kelly's gonna want her there."

Rafe touched his shoulder, squeezing in support. "Of course. I'll call Royce and King, too, and tell them what's going on. She's gonna be fine, Blade."

"Yeah." Blade stepped up into the ambulance, rushing to Kelly's side, but he wasn't fast enough.

Kelly saw the blood.

Her face lost what little color she'd had, her eyes wild with terror. "Oh my God! Blade!"

Her cry ripped at him, and with a curse, he covered her again.

Tuning out the conversation between the paramedics, Blade leaned over his wife, taking her face in his hands. "I love you, Kelly. Please calm down. I'm here. Everything will be fine."

"Oh, Blade. It's happening again."

Blade bent low, brushing her lips with his. "Calm down. You know how to do that. Breathe for me. Just focus on me and breathe. You're going to be fine."

"Blade, I'm so sorry."

Blade gripped her hand, his stomach knotted so tightly he couldn't breathe. "Sorry for what, baby?"

"I wanted so much to give you the son you wanted."

Bringing her hand to his lips, he forced a smile. "You're going to give him to me now. You just relax and breathe. We'll get to the hospital soon, and everything's going to be fine."

Gripping her chin, he purposely hardened his tone. "Have I ever lied to you, Kelly? Now, you do what I say and relax, or there'll be hell to pay when I get you back home."

To his relief, Kelly smiled. "You don't scare me anymore, tough guy." Her sob ripped through him. "I love you, Blade. If anything happens to me, I want you to know that you're everything to me."

"I love you, too, baby. You're my entire world. I promise, everything will be fine."

It had to be.

Holding her hand, he prayed like never before as they raced to the hospital, promising himself that no matter what happened, he'd never put her through this again.

Chapter Two

Kelly held on to Blade's hand like a lifeline as he ran alongside the gurney into the hospital, his presence giving her strength.

She wanted to laugh when he glared at the nurse who tried to push him aside, but another pain hit her, and she forgot all about laughing.

She squeezed his hand through it, watching the ceiling tiles whiz by until it ended. Turning her head, she met Blade's look of concern, her heart pounding faster when they turned and pushed her into a room. "It's different this time, isn't it? The pains are coming closer together, but I'm bleeding. Blade, please tell me everything'll be all right. Promise me, and no matter what, don't let go."

Blade leaned close again, brushing a hand over her hair. "Of course everything's going to be all right, and I have no intention of letting go. I'm here, honey. In a little while, we're going to have a strong son who's going to idolize his mother." His beloved features gentled, but the horror in his eyes seemed to get worse. It was so unlike him to lose his composure that she found herself trying to calm him.

Forcing a smile, she brought his hand to her lips. "Or a daughter to torment her daddy. Oh!" Clenching her jaw, she squeezed his hand again and breathed through the pain, which seemed almost never ending.

Smiling, he brought her hand to his lips again, kissing her fingers. "That's it, baby. Breathe. I swear, I won't put you through this again. I love you, Kelly. You're everything to me." He pushed her damp hair back from her forehead. "Easy, honey. I'll be with you every minute. Just try to relax."

The door opened again and there was a flurry of activity as everything seemed to happen at once.

Doctors and nurses asked all sorts of questions while changing Kelly into a gown. Monitors of every kind seemed to be everywhere.

Her doctor barked out orders like a general, while speaking to her in a low, soothing tone.

She barely felt the needle for the IV through the pain as another contraction hit her.

"Look at me." Blade's deep voice cut through the chaos surrounding her.

Responding to the steel in his tone, Kelly turned toward her husband, shocked at the change in him.

Blade appeared more like the man she'd married, the man who guided her, his strength absolute. "Focus on me. Breathe the way we practiced. In. Out. That's good. Don't pay attention to them. Pay attention to me."

"She's losing too much blood. The baby's head is out. Come on, Kelly. Push." The doctor's voice held a hint of urgency that she remembered from the past, one that sent a surge of alarm through her.

Kelly started to turn toward the doctor, but Blade stopped her, cupping her jaw and turning her face toward his. "Look at me. Come on, baby. Push. You can do it. Come on, baby. Kelly?"

His face started to swim and fade. She tried to push, but couldn't find the strength. "Blade?"

A nurse pushed on her stomach, but she didn't even have the energy to tighten against it. She lay there—feeling—but not feeling.

"Kelly? Kelly?" Blade's voice seemed to come from a great distance.

She tried to open her eyes, not even realizing when they'd closed. "Love you."

"Kelly? Kelly! Something's wrong with her. Do something, damn it!"

She'd never heard such fear in Blade's voice before and tried to reach out to him, but couldn't lift her arm.

She heard Blade screaming at the doctor, but even that started to fade.

And then she heard and felt nothing.

* * * *

Blade's knees turned to rubber when he heard the baby cry, but the doctor's next words almost took him to the floor.

Fury, fear, and desperation fueled his strength, the rage and horror building inside him erupting. He gripped the doctor by the collar, shaking so badly he almost lost his grip. "What do you mean, she's in a coma? What the fuck did you do to her?"

Rafe pushed against him, placing himself between Blade and the doctor, the deputy's eyes filled with sympathy. "Calm down, Blade. Let's take this outside. You don't want to upset Kelly."

The doctor placed a hand on Blade's shoulder, the tension in his expression scaring Blade all the way to his soul. "She lost a lot of blood. She needs to rest. We're doing everything possible for her."

Rafe gripped him by the upper arms and bodily forced him from the room. "Come on. Let's get you calmed down. You're not going to be any use to Kelly, and if she wakes up and sees you like this, she's going to be frantic."

Blade couldn't see anything except Kelly.

Pale as the sheet, she appeared to be sleeping, but he knew better.

She *had* to wake up.

Furious that this could happen to someone as sweet as his wife, and terrified for her, and for himself, he picked up a chair and flung it to the far wall with a wail of grief that echoed off of the walls.

King, Royce, and Rafe surrounded him, pushing him into a chair. He didn't want to sit, but his legs didn't seem to be working.

Aware of King dropping into the seat next to him, Blade stared down at his hands, surprised to find that he couldn't stop them from shaking. "She's in a coma. I don't know what I'm going to go if she doesn't come out of it." He fisted his hands, and flexed them again, surprised that they still shook as a kind of numbness settled around him.

"I can't live without her. Nothing can happen to her. I can't live without her. She's everything to me."

Royce knelt in front of him. "Nothing's going to happen to her. Listen to me. You've got every right to fall apart out here. You've been through a lot. But, she needs you. The baby needs you. Your son."

"My son." Blade nodded, straightening. "I know. The way she looked at me—the trust in her eyes. She trusted me to make sure nothing went wrong. I let her down."

King shot to his feet. "That's bullshit! You never let her down, and she knows it. She knows you're here for her, and she knows she can count on you. She's going to be fine, Blade. You can't let yourself think anything else. We're here for you if you need it."

Royce straightened and touched his shoulder. "Someone will be out here at all times. If you need anything, or just want to talk, we'll be waiting. Can we get you anything?"

Blade lifted his head, looking from Royce to King to Rafe. "Just for Kelly to wake up. I'm going back in there." Swallowing his fear, he took a deep breath and let it out slowly, "She needs me."

He got to his feet and struggled to put one foot in front of the other, feeling as if he'd aged ten years in the last hour.

He pushed the door to her room open, his gaze going immediately to her slight form, looking small and helpless in the hospital bed.

A low light had been left on above the bed, and as he moved closer, he could see that she'd been dressed in a fresh hospital gown.

He didn't know how long he stood at the foot of the bed, just staring at her before he felt a hand on his arm.

"Blade?"

He recognized Jesse's whispered voice, but couldn't look away from Kelly. "Look at her. Look what I did to her."

Images flashed through his mind, tormenting him.

Her curvy body draped over his lap as he spanked her.

Clips on her sensitive nipples.

Bent over the padded table and tied in place as he fucked her ass.

Standing in his playroom and secured with leather straps while he used the whip on her delicate skin.

He'd been too rough with her.

He knew he'd given her pleasure, but that didn't console him now.

Running his thumb over her soft fingers, he realized that he'd expected too much of her. He'd been so obsessed with her that he'd somehow missed the signs that the lifestyle he'd led her in to had been too much for her.

"No!" Jesse leaned against his shoulder, rubbing his back. "You didn't do this to her."

Blade drew a shuddering breath. "She had a boyfriend who used to beat her, and then she married me. A Dom. She's too fucking delicate for the things I've done to her."

Jesse squeezed his arm. "You're talking nonsense. I know you're upset about this, but none of it is your fault. You've been so good to her. So good *for* her. You wouldn't hurt her. Everyone knows that for all your big talk, you baby her. Even before she got pregnant, you fussed over her, and as soon as she found out she was pregnant the first time, you've been doing your best to wrap her in cotton. You've both been through a lot, Blade. I understand why you feel the way you do now, but Kelly loves you, and she loves what you have together. Don't ruin that."

She hugged him to her. "I'm going to go get some coffee, and give you some time alone with her. I'll bring some back for you."

Blade nodded, unable to speak, the guilt overwhelming him.

The door closed behind her, leaving him alone with his wife.

He loved Kelly more than his own life, and looking at her lying pale and helpless in a hospital bed, he couldn't imagine ever taking her to the playroom again.

She needed tenderness from him. Gentleness.

"Come on, baby. Wake up. Let me see those beautiful green eyes."

Tears stung his eyes as he lifted her hand to his lips. "Please, baby. Please wake up for me. I'm so sorry. I promise, everything's going to be different from now on. Just wake up. Everything's going to be different. I promise."

Vowing to himself that he'd never put her in this kind of danger again, and that he'd never again give her even the smallest amount of pain, Blade held her hand in his and bent over her, letting the tears flow.

Chapter Three

Voices penetrated the fog surrounding Kelly, but they faded into the distance again before she could focus enough to understand them.

The next time a voice penetrated, she recognized it immediately as Blade's.

He sounded so worried—so frantic—as he begged her to open her eyes.

She tried to obey him, but her eyelids felt as if they'd been weighed down.

Every part of her felt as if she'd been weighed down.

She started sinking into the fog again, and no matter how hard she tried, she couldn't fight it.

Maybe if she rested awhile, she'd have the strength to open her eyes for Blade.

She drifted in and out of the fog, always aware of Blade's presence. Sometimes she heard voices, and at other times she didn't.

The voices came and went too far away for her to grasp.

Deep, masculine voices.

Softer, feminine voices.

All of them seemed to hold frustration, fear, and support, surrounding her in a warm sensation of safety that made it possible for her to rest again.

The voices came again—clearer this time.

The pull of them drew her out of the fog and closer to the surface.

Beloved voices.

Things seemed a little clearer this time, and she remembered those voices pulling her from the fog at short intervals.

She wanted to move, but was afraid that it would drain her energy and suck her back into the fog and the dark void beyond.

Blade. Jesse.

"Blade, you need to sleep."

Why did Jesse sound so worried and so frustrated?

"I slept."

Poor Blade.

He sounded exhausted.

"Why don't you go out with the others for a couple of minutes? Walk around a bit. Eat something."

"I'm not hungry."

"Clay and Rio went to get some more sandwiches. You need to eat something."

"I'd choke on it. Did you check on the baby?"

"Of course. He's doing fine and eating like a horse."

The baby!

Kelly moaned, struggling to get her eyes to open.

"Kelly!" Blade's voice came from much closer now, his usually silky tone harsh and filled with desperation.

Jesse's voice came from her other side. "Thank God."

Feeling his hand tighten on hers, she squeezed it, hoping to reassure him.

He sounded so frantic!

"Come on, baby. You can do it. Open those beautiful green eyes for me. I know you can do it. Come on, baby. I've been waiting for you."

His voice, still tense became low and cajoling. "Come on, baby. You can do it."

Clinging to Blade's low voice, and warmed by the hand that gripped hers, Kelly fought to open them. She got them open once, only to have them close again. She did it again, frustrated that they wouldn't stay open.

Blade leaned closer, his breath warm against her cheek. "That's my girl. You can do it. Try again for me. I'm dying to see those beautiful eyes."

Turning toward his voice, Kelly redoubled her efforts, relieved when she finally managed to open her eyes to slits.

The first thing she saw was his beautiful face. Alarmed at how haggard he appeared, she parted her lips to form his name. Disappointed that although she moved her mouth, no sound came out, she swallowed and tried again. "Blade."

It was worth it to see the relief and joy on Blade's face.

He smiled, bending to touch his lips to hers. "You scared me, baby. How are you feeling? Are you in pain?"

Alarmed to see tears in his eyes, she squeezed his hand, shocked at how much effort it took. "No."

It came out as a hoarse whisper. Clearing her throat, she tried again. "No." Thankful that her voice had gotten stronger, she tried to smile, but tears filled her eyes, making Blade's face swim out of focus. "I'm so sorry."

Jesse touched her arm from the other side, bending to kiss her hair. "I'm going to leave you two alone. I'll tell the others she's awake. I'll be right outside in the waiting room."

Wiping her tears away, Blade nodded and brought Kelly's hand to his lips. "You won't be sorry when you see our son. He's beautiful."

The rush of joy and relief that swelled inside made her dizzy. "What?"

Blade's smile brightened the room. Laughing, he wrapped his arms around her and lifted her with incredible gentleness, his arms strong and firm around her as he held her against his chest. "We have a son, baby."

He held her, rocking her in his arms. "We have a beautiful little boy who's been waiting for his mama to wake up."

Held in her husband's arms, Kelly could feel her strength growing. "You were right."

Blade smiled and kissed her forehead. "I keep telling you that I'm always right. I told you we'd have a son, and that everything would be all right. You're very lucky to have a husband who knows everything."

Kelly couldn't help but smile at the return of Blade's usual arrogance. "I can't believe it." Laughing and crying at the same time, she reached up and gripped his shirt, feeling even stronger. "What happened? Where is he?"

Leaning back, he tilted her face to his, his eyes filled with love so strong it brought tears to her eyes. "He's in the nursery. I haven't seen him since he was born, but Jesse's been with him. I didn't want to leave you. I felt like if I left, you wouldn't—" His voice broke, shocking Kelly.

"Blade?" She didn't have the strength to hold him to her the way she would have like to.

Blade's eyes filled with tears, breaking her heart. "You've been in a coma for three days, baby. You lost so much blood. I was so scared you wouldn't come back to me."

"Oh, Blade. I knew you were with me. I just couldn't seem to surface until now. I felt you. I'll always come back to you. I can't live without you."

Burying her face against his neck, she breathed in the scent of him, a scent that always settled her. Her heart raced with excitement and she couldn't stop crying. "We have a baby boy!"

Blade lifted his head, his eyes swimming with tears. "We do. Are you ready to see him?"

By the time the nurse called the doctor, and he checked her out, Kelly felt much stronger.

Between bites of food that Blade kept feeding her, Kelly couldn't stop staring at her son. "Oh, Blade, he looks just like you." Her son had the same dark skin and black hair that her husband did, the blood of his ancestors evident. "He's so beautiful."

Blade slid the spoon of yogurt between her lips. "His mother's beautiful."

Uncomfortably aware that she looked a mess, Kelly looked away and swallowed. "No, she's not. I need a shower." Looking up, she touched his jaw. "You look exhausted. I can't believe you've been sitting in that chair for three days."

Blade's eyes filled with remembered pain. "Where else would I be? Jesus, Kelly, you scared the hell out of me." He set the yogurt aside and lifted her with a gentleness that brought tears to her eyes, cuddling her and the baby close. "I thought I was going to lose you. I couldn't live without you, baby."

His voice broke, his entire body shaking against hers.

She hadn't thought her love for him could get any stronger, but the rush of love she felt for him in that moment made it difficult to breathe. "Blade, I'm so sorry to put you through that. I'm fine now. I promise."

Blade pulled her closer. "I love you, Kelly, more than anything in the world. I can't lose you."

The baby objected, letting out a cry.

Laughing as Blade pulled away, she smiled up at him. "I think he's hungry. Oh, dear. I've never done this before."

Blade had already pushed the call button and rubbed their son's belly. "We'll have the nurse help us."

Kelly blinked and tried to adjust the baby in her arms, inwardly cursing her weakness. "Us?" Grinning up at him as he stood and lowered her to the bed again, she looked from him to the baby and back again, unable to get enough of either of them.

Blade grinned back at her, looking better than he had when she woke up, but he still looked exhausted. "I don't have the breasts for it, but I'll help you all I can. We're in this together, baby."

By the time the nurse had shown her what to do, and she'd managed to nurse the baby, Kelly was exhausted. Before the kindly nurse had even placed the baby back in the bassinette, Blade had already begun tucking Kelly back under the covers.

His eyes held more than a hint of concern. "You're still weak. Go to sleep for a while."

Kelly struggled to keep her eyes open, scared that if she went to sleep, she wouldn't be able to wake up again. "But the others... I want to see Jesse and show off our son. By the way, have you changed your mind about his name?"

Blade's slow smile made her heart beat faster. "No—unless you'd like something different."

"No. He looks so much like you. I'd like him to have the name of an ancestor you admired. Hawke Royal. I like it." Her eyes started to close again.

"Good. You go to sleep. I'll go talk to the others, and then I'll be back. I'll talk to the doctor about your shower." Bending low, he kissed her forehead, her cheek, her lips. "I'll be here when you wake up, baby. Go to sleep. The doctor said you're fine now. Just sleep and get your strength back. I need you, baby, even more than I even knew."

Chapter Four

Lying back against the pillow, Kelly smiled as she watched her best friend, Jesse, coo at Hawke. "You know, I'm kind of surprised you, Clay, and Rio haven't tried for a baby."

Seated in the chair next to the bed, Jesse didn't even look up, answering in the same singsong voice she used for the baby. "I had my tubes tied long ago. I didn't want any more children with Brian, and he certainly didn't want any more. Clay, Rio and I are happy with the three we have, and it probably sounds selfish, but we want to spend as much time together as possible."

Looking up, Jesse smiled. "We consider finding each other nothing short of a miracle."

Kelly grinned, her own heart filled with love for the man she'd married. "I feel the same way. I'm so glad you and I moved here. I don't even want to think about a life without Blade in it."

Her stomach knotted as she considered the change in him. It had been almost a week since she'd woken, and a hint of fear still lingered in his eyes.

He stared into the distance a lot, and at times, there was a strange look in his eyes.

When she asked him what was wrong, he shrugged it off. Although he touched her often and couldn't seem to stay away from her from long, she noticed a distance between them that had never been there before. She tried to blame it on his fatigue, but knew it was something more. Blinking back tears, she dropped her head back on to the pillow and sighed.

"What's wrong, Kelly?"

Kelly looked toward the door, knowing Blade could come through at any minute. "Blade's different. Something's wrong and he won't talk about it."

Shaking her head, Jesse sighed. "Jesus, Kelly, you should have seen him. It took King, Royce, and Rafe to keep him from tearing the room apart when you went into a coma. When they finally got him calmed down, he just fell apart. He and I came in here to be with you. Jesus, when he cried, it broke my heart."

Getting to her feet, Jesse placed the baby back into the bassinette before sitting on the bed next to Kelly, her eyes shimmering with tears. "He didn't want to leave you alone for a minute. He wouldn't eat. He wouldn't sleep. He didn't even go to see the baby. He just sat there holding your hand and talking to you until he was hoarse. He was afraid to leave you. Kelly, I've never seen a man so broken."

"I would have been throwing furniture against the wall, too." Clay spoke from behind Jesse, making them both jump. Coming up behind his wife, he wrapped his arms around her and smiled at Kelly. Kelly blinked. "He threw furniture? My calm, always cool and in control husband threw furniture?" She couldn't even imagine Blade doing anything like that.

Clay nodded and leaned over to smile at the baby. "Yep. You can thank Royce, King, and Rafe for not letting him break more and racking up a higher bill. It took all three of them to keep him from killing the doctor after he told him you were in a coma from too much blood loss."

Running a hand over Jesse's hair, Clay stared at her, his eyes hooded. "I can't say that I blame him. If anything happened to Jesse, I wouldn't want to live."

Turning to Kelly, he smiled. "Be prepared to be wrapped in cotton and treated as though you might break. I know you'll get frustrated, but be patient with him. He's had quite a scare."

Kelly sighed, plucking at the covers. "That's what I'm afraid of. I don't want him to worry. I want things to get back to normal. We haven't had normal in a long time. He's treated me as though I'm fragile for months."

"You have been." Coming closer, Clay bent over Kelly and kissed her forehead. "Blade's scared, Kelly. That man loves you."

Kelly watched in fascination as Clay cooed over the baby, the sight of such a huge man making ridiculous noises at a newborn making Kelly laugh. "You look ridiculous."

Clay grinned. "I don't care. You *are* going to let us babysit, aren't you? Jesse already has a crib set up for him and everything."

Kelly blinked and turned to Jesse. "You're kidding."

Jesse crossed her arms over her chest and smiled. "I don't know why that would surprise you. By the way, I called your brother." She lifted a hand before Kelly could say anything. "I told Cullen about the baby and that you were fine. I didn't tell him anything else. He's going to try to get here within the next couple of weeks."

Kelly sighed and leaned back again. "Thank you. He'd worry, too."

Clay straightened to his full height of over six and a half feet tall, and went to his wife, running his hand over her hair as he smiled at Kelly. "I'm leaving. I know you two are dying to talk without any men interfering."

He touched his lips to Jesse's forehead. "Let me know when you're ready for lunch. Blade's getting something to come back here and eat with Kelly. We'll go to the restaurant next door with King and the others when you're ready."

Jesse looked up at him, the love shining in her eyes so stunning, it took Kelly's breath away.

It seemed to have the same effect on Clay.

The way they looked at each other made Kelly feel like an intruder, but she couldn't seem to look away.

Jesse smiled up at Clay, cupping his jaw in a loving gesture that made Clay's eyes light up. "You don't have to wait for me. I know you're all hungry." Leaning against Clay, Jesse met Kelly's eyes and laughed softly. "They emptied the vending machines. All three of them."

Kelly smiled as she imagined it, her eyes brimming with tears again at the thought of how many people from Desire had come to support Blade.

And to her amazement—her.

Clay rubbed a hand over Jesse's back, his eyes narrowing. "Hell, Kelly's crying. Do you want me to go get Blade?"

Kelly couldn't help but laugh at his look of panic. "No. It's these damned hormones. I'm fine. You two just look so in love, and I was thinking about how many people came to support Blade while I was in a coma, and how everyone took me in—" Embarrassed that tears started flowing again, Kelly reached for a tissue.

Clay held his hands out in front of him, his eyes going wide. "No more crying. No more. Please. I'm leaving. Jesse, fix it. Make her stop crying."

Jesse laughed. "Get out. Give us some time alone together." Laughing as he almost ran out the door, Jesse came over and sat on the bed next to Kelly.

"It's kind of funny to see a man that big get a little frazzled by a few tears, huh?" Handing Kelly another tissue, she sniffed, her eyes suspiciously moist. "Gets me every damned time. They're so softhearted when it comes to women, it makes me love them even more."

Pulling another tissue from the box, Jesse wiped her own tears. "I can't stop thinking about the way Blade looked at you. He was so scared. He held on to you, scared to let go of you. He talked to you until he lost his voice. He laid his head on the pillow beside yours and whispered to you."

Sniffing again, she stood and went to the bassinette. "He didn't even leave the room to go see the baby. He didn't eat. I came in to check on you several times and found him wrapped around you, napping with his head on the pillow next to yours. He was scared all the way to the bone, Kelly. We all were, but Blade…"

"I know." Kelly nodded, wiping away another tear. "He's been so good with me. So loving. Patient. So strong. I've been leaning on him for a long time, Jesse."

"You needed him, and it's obvious he needs you."

Kelly blew out a breath. "But, I hate that he looks at me as if he has to be careful with me all the time. He's been doing it for so long, that even now, he doesn't want me to move. Blade's been so careful with me. He hasn't even made love to me since finding out I was pregnant this time, and I know that must be hard for him."

Taking Kelly's hand in hers, Jesse smiled. "He's been scared, Kelly. Give it time. You're not ready for that anyway."

Kelly squeezed Jesse's hand. "He's changed toward me, Jesse. It scares me. Then he goes to the club and is surrounded by all those women…"

Jesse frowned and glanced toward the closed door. "You don't really think Blade would cheat on you, do you? That man's obsessed with you."

Releasing Jesse's hand, Kelly dropped back against the pillow. "No. You know what kind of man he is, Jesse. Blade has a high sex drive and doesn't understand the word vanilla. He likes it raw and wild, and can be very demanding. I'm afraid he's never going to look at me with that kind of hunger again."

Patting her hand, Jesse got to her feet again. "That's nonsense. You'll see. When you're healed, Blade will be all over you."

Hearing the door open, Kelly forced a smile. "I'm sure you're right."

Blade paused to drop a kiss on Jesse's head as he approached the bed. "Your husbands are waiting to take you out for lunch and then home. You look tired, honey, and Clay and Rio are getting a little desperate. You've been here for days."

Shaking her head, Jesse giggled, something she did with heartwarming regularity since marrying Clay and Rio. "Those two worry too much." Poking Blade in the stomach, Jesse shook her head, still smiling. "You men think we're going to break or something. Just remember, we put up with all of you on a daily basis."

Blade's jaw clenched. "You're all too fragile, and you're all too important to us. It's terrifying at times."

Kelly's stomach dropped. Shaken by the anguish in her husband's eyes, she shared a look with Jesse as Hawke began to cry, drawing Blade's attention.

Jesse smiled reassuringly before saying her good-byes. "I'll stop in again tomorrow morning before work. I know they're planning to release you tomorrow, so I'll see you again tomorrow night. It sounds like Hawke's hungry."

Blade lifted his son from the bassinette. "Hungry, huh? I guess mommy's breasts are yours for now, little guy." He placed the baby in Kelly's arms and sat beside her, supporting her weight with a strong arm wrapped around her back.

Wincing when Hawke latched on, Kelly leaned back against her husband. "I hope you don't forget that they're yours, too."

"Hmm." Blade kissed her hair. "Right now, you just worry about getting your strength back."

Kelly sighed and let her eyes flutter closed, hating feeling so weak. She could only hope that Jesse was right. The almost desperate need to have proof that things would be the same as before ate at her.

He'd gotten so used to babying her and treating her with kid gloves that she feared he'd never see her the same way again.

She knew that neither one of them could live with that.

Chapter Five

Blade sat in the cafeteria sipping coffee with his friends while several of the women from Desire visited with Kelly.

Three other tables had been pushed together to accommodate everyone.

"You look like hell." Rio slapped his back as he made his way to the seat next to him. "Have you slept at all?"

Scrubbing a hand over his face, Blade nodded. "Yeah. I sleep in the chair in Kelly's room."

Sitting across from Blade, King shook his head, his eyes dark with concern. "He won't even go home to shower. Royce and I brought a couple of changes of clothes in here so he could shower in Kelly's room."

Blade sighed, staring into his cup. "I'm scared to leave her." His voice sounded raw and hoarse to his own ears. He was exhausted, but couldn't seem to sleep more than an hour at a time, spending most of the night staring at Kelly and listening to her breathe. He lived on sandwiches in her room because he didn't want to leave her long enough to get something else. Today was the first time he sat in the cafeteria, and only did so because he knew Kelly was surrounded by her friends—women who would watch over her, and fuss over her and the baby.

Chase, who sat at the other end of the table, bounced his and Boone's daughter, Theresa, on his lap. "I remember that feeling. After seeing Rachel give birth, I swore I was never going to touch her again. Boone and I told her we were going to get vasectomies because we never wanted to see her go through that kind of pain again."

Blade looked up. "I've decided the same thing. I have an appointment in two weeks."

Chase shrugged. "As long as you and Kelly agree."

Pushing the guilt aside, Blade clenched his jaw. "I haven't told her. It's my decision."

The silence that followed as the men all looked at each other had Blade glancing around the table. "Why are all of you looking at me like that?" Looking from Chase to Boone, he shrugged. "You know what it feels like. Christ, Kelly's been through enough, don't you think?"

Jared, Duncan, and Reese looked more than a little uncomfortable. Their own wife, Erin, was due in less than two months. Grimacing, Jared shook his head. "I have to admit, I'm scared to death. Imagining Erin in pain has given me a hell of a lot of sleepless nights."

He shared a look with his brothers. "But, I wouldn't think about doing something as drastic as a vasectomy without talking to Erin. I don't think Kelly would appreciate that you made that kind of decision for her."

Shaking his head, Blade stared down into his coffee, his stomach burning. "I can't let her go through this again. I just can't. Two miscarriages. She was so lost, and looked at me like she'd disappointed me somehow. She's so damned fragile. I didn't want to try again, but she insisted. I don't think I've stopped shaking since she told me she was pregnant again. At the house…God, there was blood everywhere."

Jake Langley laid a hand on Blade's shoulder. "Rafe told us. He also told us what happened when Kelly slipped into a coma." He squeezed Blade's shoulder in sympathy. "But, Blade, Kelly's fine. The doctor said the blood loss caused the coma, but she's fine now. She's going home tomorrow, isn't she? She's just going to be weak for a little while, but I know the girls are already making schedules to come and help her."

Blade nodded, relieved that he would soon have Kelly and the baby home. "Yeah. She and the baby are coming home. She's so weak, though. The doctor said it's going to take several weeks for her to get her strength back. She's so little. So delicate. When she was in a coma, I sat there staring at her, holding her hand—*willing* her to come back. I could have lost her." Getting to his feet, he raked a hand through his hair. "If she's angry about the vasectomy, I'll deal with it. I'd rather have her mad at me than risk losing her again."

He blew out a breath, scrubbing a hand over his face. "I'll make her understand. Once she's had a chance to rest and heal, I'll tell her."

He wanted his wife safe and healthy. Nothing else mattered.

Clay touched his shoulder. "Blade, let's take a walk."

Intrigued by Clay's tone, Blade felt the stirring of panic at the thought that Jesse might have said something about Kelly. "What is it? Did you hear something about Kelly?"

Clay gripped his arm, grabbing Blade's shirt when he would have shrugged him off. "No. Nothing like that. Come on. Let's take a walk outside. I want to talk to you about something Jesse told me."

Blade relaxed, but only marginally. "What is it? You wouldn't be breaking Jesse's confidence if it wasn't important."

Clay grinned. "I wouldn't break Jesse's confidence unless it was life or death. No, this is something she wanted me to pass along to you, but she'd appreciate it, and so would I, if you didn't tell Kelly that we had this conversation."

"That depends." Blade walked with Clay down the hall and toward the elevator. "I don't like keeping secrets from Kelly any more than you like keeping them from Jesse."

Clay nodded. "Fair enough." The crowd of people in the elevator ended the conversation, a conversation that didn't resume until they'd stepped outside and made their way to a deserted area.

Worried about what Clay had to say and impatient to get back to Kelly, Blade stopped, spinning back to face his friend. "Okay, what does Jesse want me to know?"

Leaning back against one of the trees, Clay smiled faintly. "She's concerned about Kelly, and she's concerned about you. Jesse knows how much you love Kelly, but she also knows—her words—*how you Neanderthals think.*"

Blade lifted his brows at that, but waited for Clay to continue.

Chuckling softly, Clay shrugged. "She's right. She usually is, but don't tell her I said that. She said that you're so determined to wrap Kelly in cotton that you don't see that Kelly's scared she's losing you."

Stunned, Blade stiffened. "What? That's ridiculous. Kelly wouldn't think any such thing. Jesse must be mistaken."

Clay nodded, obviously expecting such a reaction. "She said that Kelly's worried because after the miscarriages, you've been babying her throughout her pregnancy. After what happened during delivery, it's even worse. She's afraid that you've become so used to handling her with kid gloves that things won't go back to the way they used to be. She's afraid you'll never see her as anything other than delicate and a mother to Hawke, not as a desirable woman." Clearing his throat, Clay shrugged, looking decidedly uncomfortable.

"Look, I don't want to get into this, and I wouldn't if Jesse hadn't asked me to, but Kelly seems concerned that you spend a lot of time at the club with beautiful women, women who would be glad to give you what you won't go to her for."

"That's ridiculous. I couldn't even think about touching another woman."

"I know that, and you know that, but Kelly's really upset about it."

Blade inwardly winced, hurting for his wife, but unable to imagine taking her back into the playroom after what she'd been through. "Thanks. I'll figure it out."

He didn't know how, but he'd think of a way to appease his wife, and assure her that he had no interest in any other woman.

If she was too fragile for the playroom, he could do without it.

Walking back toward the hospital entrance with Clay alongside him, Blade looked up toward Kelly's room. "I'll dismantle the playroom. I'll convince her that I'm not interested in having one anymore."

Clay whipped his head around. "I think you're making a mistake." With a sigh, he met Blade's glare. "But it's your wife." Slapping him on the back, he gestured for Blade to precede him. "If you piss her off, we're both going to regret it."

Walking inside, Blade looked back at Clay over his shoulder, hurrying his steps as the need to get to Kelly became overwhelming. "I don't care about pissing her off. She'll get over it. As long as she's safe and healthy. Nothing's more important to me than that."

He paused, turning to Clay. "I almost lost her. I could have lost her. I can't handle that again. She's everything to me. Tell me, honestly, that if you had a choice of endangering Jesse's life, or pissing her off, which choice would you make?"

Clay inclined his head. "I'd piss her off, which I assume is what's going to happen with Kelly, but taking her into your playroom isn't endangering her life. So, let me ask you something."

He turned to look around them before leaning close. "If you have a choice of doing what both you and your wife desperately need, or making her feel as if you don't desire her the way you used to, which choice would you make?"

"Damn it, Clay. It's not like that!"

Clay's brow went up. "From where I'm standing, it's exactly like that."

Blade cursed, the mental image of Kelly lying pale and unconscious in bed layered over the image of her writhing on the padded table in the playroom making him break out in a cold sweat.

"I can't. I just can't. She's so damned fragile."

Blade pushed the image aside and walked away.

He didn't need to dominate Kelly. Their sex life could survive without it.

He'd give her so much love and affection that she wouldn't even miss it.

Chapter Six

Kelly placed the baby back in the bassinette and went in search of Blade. They'd arrived home from the hospital just over an hour ago, and although she hated to admit it, she was ready for a nap.

Despite her protests, he'd carried her and the baby into the house, and gotten them settled, only to disappear soon afterward. Figuring he'd gone into his office to catch up on some work, she grabbed the baby monitor and headed in that direction.

She moved carefully down the stairs, pleased at how quickly she'd begun to regain her strength. Grinning at the thought of getting back into shape and seducing her husband, Kelly turned left at the bottom of the stairway, anxious to see Blade.

Her smile fell as she went through the doorway, and surprised to find the room empty, she frowned and turned around. Retracing her steps, she went back toward the living room, stilling when she heard a sound coming from upstairs.

Wondering what he could be doing, she went back up the stairs again, checking on the baby as she passed the master bedroom.

Pausing, she listened, shocked that the sounds she heard came from the playroom located off of their bedroom. With an uneasy feeling in the pit of her stomach, she slowed her steps, and paused outside a door that only Blade opened. For the first time, she reached for the knob, some instinct urging her on.

Swinging the door open, she stepped inside, her stomach knotting when she saw that half of the cabinets had been emptied and several boxes sat open on the padded table.

Blade swung toward her, his eyes full of concern. "What's wrong, baby? Look at you." In a few long strides he was at her side, his arms going around her to pull her against him. "You're exhausted. I thought you were going to bed as soon as you fed Hawke."

"I missed you." She gestured toward the boxes, some of them still open. "What are you doing?"

Turning her away from the room and toward the doorway, Blade kissed her hair. "Just cleaning the room out a little. Nothing for you to worry about. Come on. The doctor said you need plenty of rest."

Kelly tried to push out of his arms, but he held firm. "Blade, I don't like this. Why are you putting the things from the playroom away? I'll be back to myself in no time."

With a curse, Blade lifted her, his hold gentle, but firm as he turned and left the room, cradling her against his chest. "You're weak as a newborn kitten. The doctor released you because he knew I would take care of you. That means making sure that you get the rest you need."

Kelly panicked, feeling as if her world was crumbling around her. She didn't like the pinched look in Blade's expression as he strode down the hall and into their bedroom. "Please, Blade. Don't get rid of the playroom. You and I both need—"

Blade paused next to the bed, setting her on her feet and removing her robe with an ease that brought back memories of the times that he'd stripped her in the past.

His haunted expression made the knots in her stomach even tighter and sent a shiver of fear through her. "No, Kelly. I don't *need* the playroom. What I *need*, Kelly, is you in my life. Safe. Healthy. Happy. I don't need the playroom. I need *you*." He settled her into bed, easily overcoming her resistance. Tucking her in, he took the monitor from her. "I'll listen for the baby. You just get some sleep."

Gripping his arm as he turned away, Kelly blinked back tears at the thought of her marriage crumbling all around her. "Blade, please listen to me. I need you, too. I need the man I married. I need it to be the way it was before. If you get rid of the playroom, you're ruining everything."

Easing his long frame to the bed, he sat beside her, his reassuring smile doing nothing to reassure her. "You're distraught, and so tired you're not making sense. Get some sleep. We'll talk about this later."

"But, Blade—"

"No!" Jumping to his feet, Blade clenched his fists at his side, blowing out a breath as he thrust a hand through his hair. "Kelly, just let it go. I can't go through it again. I almost lost you. Don't ask me to risk going through that ever again. Get some sleep."

Struggling to a sitting position, Kelly held up a hand. "Blade!"

Turning back to her, Blade clenched his jaw, his eyes tortured. "What is it, baby?"

Blinking back the tears that clouded her vision, she reached out a hand to him. "Don't do this to us, Blade. Please."

Taking her hand, he bent and touched his lips to the backs of her fingers. "I'm doing this *for* us, Kelly. Go to sleep. I need you healed and healthy again."

"And I need *you*. I need my husband back."

Blade's slow smile alarmed her. "You've got me. Always. But I can't bear the thought of losing you. We came too close, Kelly. Too close. I can't go through that ever again."

Forcing a calmness into her tone that she didn't feel, Kelly tried to get through to him. "Blade, I know you were scared, but what happened has nothing to do with the playroom. Please, Blade. I'm begging you."

Bending t touch his lips to hers, Blade settled her back in bed and pulled the covers over her. "I don't want you to worry about a thing. Just get some rest. Everything's going to be fine. You'll see."

Watching him go, Kelly wasn't so sure.

She had several weeks to convince him, though, and could only hope that once he got over his fear, everything would be back to normal.

* * * *

Blade couldn't tear his eyes away from his wife.

His cock throbbed with need for her, a need he knew would have to go unsatisfied for several more weeks.

Since having the baby, she seemed even more lush and voluptuous than ever.

There was a wicked look in her eyes now, one that he'd seen more than once, as if she had plans for him that he didn't know about.

Fighting the urge to gather her against him and force it out of her, he sipped at his coffee and tried to pretend he didn't want her naked and over his lap.

He took a sip of coffee, eyeing her over the rim of the cup. "You've lost quite a bit of weight since having Hawke. Are you sure you're not overdoing it?"

He loved her curves, but her smaller waist now made her swollen breasts look even larger. His palms itched to cup them, to feel her nipple pebble against his hand. Her hips begged for his touch, and just the thought of closing his hands on them and thrusting into her from behind had his cock leaking moisture.

She gave him one of the saucy grins that sent a surge of heat to his cock as she leaned over to refill his cup, giving him a tantalizing view of her cleavage. "Not at all. The doctor's very pleased with my progress. He said that I'm doing amazingly well, and said that I'm a strong woman."

Straightening, she ran a soft hand over his clenched jaw. "But you already know that, don't you?"

Blade narrowed his eyes, knowing damned well what she was up to. "You're strong in some aspects, but physically, you're very fragile." Ignoring his coffee, he shot to his feet. "I've got to get to the club. There are a lot of registrations for the next group of seminars that I have to go through."

With the intention of giving her a quick kiss and getting the hell out of there before he did something stupid, Blade gathered her close from behind, unable to resist burying his face against her soft neck and breathing in the scent of her. "Make sure you get some rest today. You look a little tired."

"I'm not tired, Blade, and you know it. Besides, it's never a nice thing to tell a woman she looks tired." Reaching back, she cupped the bulge at the front of his dark trousers. "Did you think you could hide this from me?"

Blade groaned, grabbing her wrist and yanking her hand away. "You know damned well that you can't make love for several more weeks."

Turning in his arms, she lifted her hands to tease the ends of his ink-black hair and rub against him, looking up at him through her lashes. "That doesn't mean I can't please you." Dropping to her knees in front of him, she reached for the fastening of his pants.

* * * *

"No!" Blade yanked her back up again, his breathing much harsher. His eyes had a wildness to them that Kelly couldn't wait to explore. "You're not sucking my cock, damn it!"

Smiling to hide the turmoil raging inside her, Kelly ran her hands over his chest. "You used to love to make me suck your cock. You liked when I got on my knees."

Spurred on when his eyes narrowed and began to glitter, Kelly hid a smile and pressed her pebbled nipples against his chest. "You used to like holding my head, and fucking my mouth. It always made me crazy when you made me keep my legs parted. How did you know that I was trying to rub my clit against my foot?"

Blade swallowed heavily. "Because I watched you. I always knew everything that you were doing. I knew what you were feeling. Your eyes always give you away, baby."

Teasing his nipples, she rubbed her belly against his cock, thrilled at his sharp intake of breath. "Then you should know what I'm feeling now. I want to please my husband. I want my Master back."

Gripping her upper arms, Blade set her away from him, his breathing harsh and his hooded eyes nearly black. "I know what you want. Your Master never left you. I do what *I* want to do to you. It's up to *me*, remember? I'm the one in control, and you have to take what I give you—*when* I decide to give it to you."

He ran a hand over her back to her bottom, sending a delicious shiver through her. "This is my body to use as I wish, and you have no say in it. I want you to get some rest, and you'd better not disobey me!"

Smiling, Kelly cupped his tight butt. "And what are you going to do to me if I don't?"

A muscle worked in his jaw as he reached behind him and took her wrists in his. "Don't push me on this, Kelly. We'll make love as soon as the doctor gives the okay. Until then, behave yourself."

Kelly grinned. "Or what, Master?"

With a growl, Blade dropped a quick kiss on her forehead and released her. "Don't push me, Kelly. Go take a nap. I'll probably be late, but I'll call to make sure you ate dinner. If you need something, call me."

Kelly watched him go, waiting until the door closed behind him before she dropped into the chair he'd just vacated. "Don't push you, huh? You just wait until I get the all clear from the doctor. Then you're going to see how far I can push."

After checking on Hawke, Kelly changed into her workout clothes and began to stretch, determined that by the time the doctor gave the okay again, Blade wouldn't know what hit him.

Chapter Seven

Trembling with excitement, Kelly turned to admire herself in the large bathroom mirror, knowing she'd never looked so good. She'd worked hard to lose the baby weight, and had been surprised at how well her new diet and exercise routine had helped her not only get rid of the pounds, but had shaped her body into one that she'd never had before.

Her new red nightgown looked good on her, the soft lace hugging her new curves to perfection. The peekaboo lace let her nipples show, as well as her freshly waxed mound.

She'd layered the vanilla scent she loved so much over her entire body, the rich moisturizer making her body glow.

She looked fantastic and had never felt better in her life.

She fluffed her hair, admiring her new haircut, the layered style framing her face and making her eyes look even bigger. The blonde highlights brightened her face and the tousled style made her look even sexier.

"Kelly, are you okay?" Blade's tense voice came from the bedroom.

Grinning, Kelly smoothed on a lip stain that darkened her lips and made them look as if she'd been kissed. "I'm fine, Blade. I'll be out in a minute."

She knew how much Blade liked the pink stain. She'd gotten it over a week ago, and every time she wore it, he stared at her lips as if he wanted to take a bite.

Tonight, she'd need every advantage she could get.

Turning again, she stood on her toes to make sure that she looked her best from all angles, stilling at the knock on the bathroom door.

"You've been in there a long time."

Reining in her grin, she adopted a small polite smile and swung the door open, almost swallowing her tongue at the sight of Blade's bare chest and disheveled hair as if he'd run his fingers through it countless times. "I'm sorry. Did you need to use the bathroom?"

His eyes went wide as they raked over her and then narrowed when they settled on her face again. "I was getting worried. Are you okay?"

Kelly snuggled against him, smiling at the feel of his cock jumping against her belly. "I feel great."

Wearing nothing but black cotton pants, which rode low on his flat stomach, Blade looked sexy as hell. He looked dark and exotic and smelled like heaven.

Turning her head, she pressed her lips against his chest and breathed the warm scent of him, thrilled at the feel of his hands clenching on her upper arms.

He wanted her. Badly.

She could feel the sexual tension pulsating all around him.

Just thinking about tonight had kept her aroused all day, and finally being in Blade's arms sent her arousal soaring.

Her nipples tightened almost painfully, the friction of the soft lace against them and the heat of his chest making the sensation even stronger.

It had been a long time since he'd touched her sexually, and her clit tingled with anticipation.

Her pussy clenched with the need for him, releasing a rush of moisture that coated her inner thighs.

Lifting her head, Kelly cupped his cheek and smiled. "I went to the doctor's today."

Blade's eyes hardened, and he went stiff. "What did he say? What happened? I knew something was wrong."

"Blade. Stop it. I didn't tell you I was going because I know how nervous you get." She rubbed against him. "I had my checkup, and so did Hawke. The doctor is very pleased with how we're both doing. Hawke gained another pound."

Blade smiled. "Good. He eats enough." His eyes narrowed. "What did he say about you? Is it too much on you?"

Kelly smiled and shook her head, determined to get her hardheaded husband to see that she was no longer the pale, weak woman lying in a hospital bed. "He says that I'm fine and I can resume all normal activities—including making love with my husband."

To her surprise, Blade didn't seem thrilled with the news.

His eyes narrowed even more, and he stepped back, gripping her shoulders and putting several inches between them. "You're not ready for that. Come on. You must be tired. Let's get you into bed so you can get some sleep before Hawke wakes up to eat again."

Losing patience, Kelly blew out a breath and tried to close the distance between them again, but Blade didn't let her. "Blade, the doctor says I'm ready. I'm fine. Better than ever. I'm a healthy woman and I want my husband."

Blade scraped a hand through his hair. "I can't. I'm too scared of hurting you."

Kelly smiled, rubbing a hand over his chest. "I know you're probably worried about getting me pregnant again, but we'll use a condom, or I can ask the doctor for pills."

"No, damn it! You're not taking any fucking pills!"

Kelly blinked as Blade turned away and strode to the window, his entire body tense as he braced himself against the wall. "What the hell's wrong with you?"

Shaking his head, he slumped. "Nothing. Just tired. Go to bed, Kelly."

Approaching him from behind, Kelly kept her voice low and seductive, trying to hide the fear that her husband no longer wanted her. "I don't want to go to bed without you. I want you to take me. It's been so long, Blade." She ran her hands over his back as she closed in, running them around to his stomach as she pressed her face against the hard lines of his back. "I need you." Sliding her hands lower, she cupped his cock through his soft pants, smiling to find him even harder than before.

His reaction, though, was more than she'd bargained for.

He cursed and jerked away from her as if she'd touched him with a live wire. "I said, no, damn it!"

Shaken, and trying her best to hold back tears, Kelly wrapped her arms around herself, suddenly chilled. "But you want me. You're aroused."

Blade turned to look at her over his shoulder, his features harder and colder than she'd ever seen them. "I'm in charge of my arousal. It doesn't control me."

Lifting her chin, Kelly swallowed the lump in her throat and voiced her inner fear. "So, you're aroused, but you don't want *me* anymore. I'm a mother now, not like those skinny young things that parade naked around the club. You're turned off that my breasts are always leaking milk, and—"

Blade whipped around, his expression one of fury. He opened his mouth as if to say something, but thought better of it. Fisting his hands at his sides, he turned away again. "That's the stupidest thing I've ever heard you say."

Kelly ran up to him, tired of talking to his back. Grabbing his shoulder, she turned him toward her. "Oh, now I'm being ridiculous. I want to make love with my husband and I'm being ridiculous? You're the one who's being ridiculous."

Blade took a deep breath and let it out slowly, his expression softening. "That's enough, honey." He gathered her against him, running his hands up and down her back. "You're getting yourself all worked up for nothing. Calm down."

Kelly shoved at him, knowing that the only reason she could move him was because he allowed it. "Over nothing? Don't you fucking tell me to calm down." Fisting her hands on her hips, she released the hold on her temper, knowing that if she didn't give full rein to it, she'd end up crying. "What's going on, Blade? You get yourself another woman while I've been out of commission?"

Blade blinked, as if he hadn't been expecting that. "Don't be ridiculous."

Incensed, she slapped at him, something that the old Blade would have never allowed. "You call me ridiculous one more time and I'm going to punch you."

She wanted to cry. She wanted to curl up in bed and sob until she didn't have any tears left.

Blade didn't want her anymore.

Gathering her close again, Blade kissed her hair. "See, now you've gotten yourself all worked up. That's not good for you. You need to settle down."

Overcoming her struggles, he lifted her high against his chest. "I love you, baby. I can't stand to see you like this. Just calm down. Everything's going to be all right. I don't have another woman. The only woman I want is you. You're getting yourself all worked up over nothing." Lowering her to the bed, he brushed his lips over her jaw. "That's my girl."

Kelly fought the surge of lust that swept through her at his soft, silky tone, a tone her body knew well and responded to without hesitation. "I'm worked up because I'm horny and my own husband doesn't want to fuck me."

Lifting his head, Blade smiled, all trace of anger gone. "Poor baby. You always get mad when you're aroused. I'll take care of that for you."

Struggling to catch up with his sudden mood shift, Kelly stared up at him. "Blade, I want you to make love to me."

Arching as he slid his hand to the neckline of her nightgown, she smiled, relieved that she'd finally gotten through to him. She gasped as he tightened his hold and tugged, ripping the delicate nightgown from her with an ease that stunned her.

Aroused her.

Reaching for him, she spread her thighs, anxious for him to take her. It had been far too long since she'd felt him thick and hot inside her. "Thank God."

Blade's smile held the hint of arrogance she'd always loved, but also more than a little bit of tension. Gathering both of her wrists in one of his strong hands, he lifted her arms over her head, his eyes raking over her. "Beautiful."

Moving to kneel between her thighs, he spread them wider, his free hand moving to her breast. "Look at you."

Thrilled at the hunger in his eyes, Kelly arched against him. "Take me, Blade."

Tracing his finger over the drop of milk on her nipple, he smoothed it over her breast. "So fucking beautiful. So soft. So delicate."

Sucking in a breath at the feel of her husband's hand moving slowly down the center of her body, Kelly moaned and bit her lip as her stomach muscles quivered under his touch. "Please. Don't make me wait. Please, Blade."

Her pussy clenched with need for him, the anticipation making her crazy. Jolting at the slide of his thumb over her swollen and aching clit, Kelly gasped and fought to get her hands free, elated and more aroused at the knowledge that she couldn't.

It had been so long since he'd held her with such firmness, or looked at her with such hunger. Burning for him, she fought his hold in her need to get closer, the slide of his thumb over her clit pushing her closer and closer to the edge.

"Take me. Fuck me, damn you! I don't want to come like this. I want to come with you inside me." She didn't want to come without the closeness of having her husband inside her. She wanted his heat and strength surrounding her.

Using his muscular thighs to keep hers parted, Blade stared down at her, watching her closely as he continued to manipulate her clit. "You're not ready for that. Shh. There, baby. Doesn't that feel good?"

"Blade! Damn it. Fuck me!"

"No, baby." The silkiness in his tone, his strong hold and the expertise in his touch as he slid his finger back and forth over her clit had her writhing beneath him in an attempt to hold off her orgasm.

Of course, with Blade, the effort proved useless.

Taking her mouth in a slow kiss, one filled with love and possessiveness, he sent her over with a speed and skill that left her breathless, her body arching and tightening as the waves of tingling heat washed over her.

Lifting his head, he smiled down at her. "That's my girl. God, I love to watch you come."

Releasing her hands, he gathered her against him. "You're so beautiful. I love you so much, baby." He buried his face in her hair, pressing his lips against her neck, her shoulder, her jaw.

Wrapping her legs around him, Kelly pressed her mound against his still-hard cock. "Blade, I want you. It's okay to take me. Please."

Lifting his head, he pushed her hair back, holding her the way he always did to settle her. "Not tonight, honey. Shh. You need your sleep. I love you, Kelly." His eyes glittered with an emotion so strong, it took her breath away.

"Nothing's as important to me as keeping you safe. I swear, I'll do everything in my power to make sure you're never hurt again." He took her mouth in another searing kiss, sending sharp pleasure through her.

Lifting his head again, he got up from the bed and pulled the covers over her. "Never. I need you too much. Go to sleep, baby."

Panicked, Kelly gripped his arm. "Where are you going?"

Blade smiled and kissed her hand before turning off the light. "I'm going to check on Hawke and do a little more work on the computer. I came home early because I missed you and I have some things to finish up."

Lying in the darkness, Kelly listened to the door close, her body still humming from her orgasm.

It wasn't enough.

She wanted Blade. She *needed* Blade.

For the first time since she met him, he seemed so far out of reach to her.

She missed her husband. She missed her tender lover.

She missed her Master.

Wiping away a tear, she turned to her side and hugged the pillow.

She couldn't let this go on. She had to find a way to get him back to the man he used to be.

If what she had with Blade died, a part of her would die with it.

She couldn't let a part of him die, too.

Something had to be done.

And soon.

* * * *

Blade went out the front door and to his car, pausing to lean against the door frame.

Hell, he was close to coming in his fucking pants!

Kelly was driving him crazy.

He wanted her so much that he couldn't even sleep at night, and no amount of jerking off helped.

He wanted *her*.

Every day, she was stronger and sexier than the day before.

She'd always been self-conscious about her weight, but he'd assured her that he loved her just the way she was.

Since having the baby, she'd been on a diet and exercise routine that had not only reshaped her body, but herself.

She had a confidence about her since giving birth that she hadn't had before, a confidence that seemed to grow as her body got smaller.

And as her arousal grew.

He should have known that the passion she'd learned to embrace would demand to be set free.

He opened his car door, only to slam it shut again, and started walking to the club, hoping the walk would help him get rid of some of this tension.

After seeing her in the hospital, he never thought he'd imagine dominating her again, but as her confidence and daring grew, so did his need to have her submission.

The challenge in her eyes stroked the dominant side of him, pushing his control to its limits. He wanted her with a hunger like never before.

He wanted to push the boundaries of her submission until he wiped that daring and hurt from her eyes, and replaced it with satisfaction and wonder beyond what she'd ever experienced.

Every day, it got harder and harder to resist her, and he knew it was only a matter of time before his control snapped and he took what belonged to him.

Tender domination.

He could make her come over and over, and satisfy her need to submit, but he could do it with tenderness.

Hopefully, it would get her to stop daring him so often, her defiance and the way she wiggled that ass testing his patience.

And if she had any more of those sexy nightgowns, he'd just have to rip them up, too.

Blowing out a breath, he continued down the street to the club, so deep in thought that he was walking up the stairs to the entrance of the club before he knew it.

He went straight to his office and sat down, staring at the computer screen.

He couldn't stop thinking about the toys he'd packed in boxes and stored in the attic. Each one had brought back memories that even now had his cock standing at attention.

He couldn't go into one of the playrooms without thinking about his own playroom at home, and the things he'd done to his beloved and sassy wife.

Another seminar approached, and he couldn't imagine training Masters while not thinking about doing the same things to Kelly.

He had to do something about his wife soon.

Before she drove him mad.

Chapter Eight

A week later, still frustrated, Kelly lay back against the pillows, waiting for Blade to get out of the shower.

Since the night she'd begged him to take her, he'd been loving and solicitous, and so sweet she wanted to smack him.

She knew he loved her. She knew he was scared, but she had the feeling that if she let this go on too long, it would become permanent, and she didn't think either one of them could live with that.

She'd flirted and thrown herself at him all week, and although the tension between them got stronger by the day, he still hadn't made love to her.

Deciding that he was afraid to get her pregnant again, she'd gone to see the doctor and gotten a prescription for birth control pills.

She'd gotten it filled, but hadn't taken any yet. The doctor had advised her not to take them while nursing Hawke, and she didn't want to give up nursing just yet.

Still, she wanted her husband back.

She stiffened as the bathroom door open, her stomach clenching at the picture Blade made as he walked into the bedroom, a cloud of steam behind him.

With a towel wrapped around his waist, he used another to rub his hair dry, the dampness from the shower still gleaming on his dark chest.

Pausing when he saw her, he smiled and tossed the towel over his shoulder. "Hey, baby. Is everything okay?"

Kelly shrugged, letting her eyes feast on him. "I need to talk to you about something."

Pushing his hair back with his fingers, he moved to stand at the foot of the bed, once again keeping distance between them. "What is it? Is something wrong? I know you went back to the doctor's today. What did he say?"

Crossing her arms over her chest, Kelly leaned back and smiled. "I realized that you weren't making love to me because you're scared I'll get pregnant again. I asked him for some pills."

Blade's features hardened. "No. I told you that you're not taking any pills."

"Blade, listen. If I start taking the pills, I'll have to put Hawke on formula, but—"

"No!" Shaking his head, Blade came around the bed and sat next to her. Blowing out a breath, he took her hand in his and smiled, a smile that didn't quite reach his eyes. "No, baby. I don't want you taking pills and I want you to keep nursing Hawke for as long as you want to."

Wrapping an arm around her, he hugged her. "I love watching you with him."

Gripping her jaw, he tilted her head back over his arm and touched his lips to hers. "I love both of you so damned much."

Kelly froze as his hand slid to her breast, not daring to believe that he was finally going to make love to her again.

Lifting his head, Blade smiled. "You're so lush, that sometimes I just want to take a bite out of you."

Loving the feel of her husband's touch, Kelly turned toward him, lifting her hands to thread her fingers through his damp hair. "Be my guest."

Blade's smile held a hint of devious intention that she hadn't seen in a long time. Fisting his hand in her hair, he pulled her head back for a long, lingering kiss, one that had a possessiveness and demand for her surrender that had been absent for a long time.

Her body and mind responded immediately—having already been trained to know the pleasure that would follow.

The feel of his hand sliding into her nightgown and over her breast sent a sharp stab of pleasure to her clit and pussy, a pleasure she'd waited months for. "Yes. Oh, God, Blade. Touch me the way you used to. I miss it so much."

Stilling at the demanding cry from the bassinette in the corner, Kelly moaned in frustration. "Damn it, Blade. You'd better not forget where we left off."

Blade's soft chuckle against her neck sent a shiver of delight through her. "Not a chance. I'm not going anywhere. I'm going to feed my son tonight."

Kelly giggled. "That would be a neat trick."

With a quick jerk, he yanked her nightgown to her waist, cupping her swollen breasts and lifting them. "These are mine—or have you forgotten?"

Trembling with hunger at the steel in his tone, Kelly watched him with their son.

His soft, deep tone caught her son's attention at once and cut off his cries.

Smiling as he changed Hawke's diaper as if he'd done it for years, Kelly brought her knees to her chest and wound her arms around them. "He always stops crying when you speak to him."

Blade lifted a brow and turned toward her, the faint smile playing at his lips filled with pride. "He knows who his father is, and he's smart enough to know who's in charge."

After dressing Hawke again and washing his hands, Blade gathered his son against his chest and strode toward her.

Kelly opened her arms for Hawke, smiling at him as Blade moved to sit behind her. Unsurprised when Hawke started crying again, she started to cup her breast, startled when Blade drew her hand away.

"I told you that I would feed him. You just hold Hawke."

Cradling Hawke with one arm, he cupped her breast with the other, lifting her nipple to her son's mouth, chuckling when he latched on. "He's really hungry, isn't he?"

Leaning back against Blade, Kelly closed her eyes, loving the feel of her husband's arms around her.

Loving his possessiveness.

"Yes, your darling son is becoming a little pig." She opened her eyes and stared down at Hawke, smiling to find him watching her. Love for him gripped her by the throat. "The doctor is thrilled with how well he's doing. He said that he doesn't look like any preemie he's ever seen."

Blade's arms tightened around her. "I know. I called him to check on both of you. He wants you to continue breast feeding as long as possible."

"Yes." Kelly looked up at him over her shoulder, reaching up to cup his jaw. "I'm sorry. I know that you're worried about making love to me because you don't want me to get pregnant again—"

"There's no risk of that."

Struck by something in his tone, Kelly frowned, an uneasy feeling settling in the pit of her stomach. "What do you mean by that?"

Stroking a finger over Hawke's cheek, he stiffened against her. "I had a vasectomy."

"What?" Whipping her head around, she stiffened, hardly able to believe she'd heard him right.

Blade's arms tightened around her, his voice taking on that steely firmness she knew so well. "You heard me. I'm not taking the chance of losing you again."

"Blade! I can't believe you would do that. We wanted more children. We talked about having two or three." Sad, angry, and hurt, she shook her head, looking away. "I can't believe you would do something like that without talking to me first. Don't you want any more children?"

"No. Not if having them is going to put your life in jeopardy." Kissing her hair, he held her close. "Look at what you've been through. I love you too much to risk it. The doctor told you it would be a risk to have another child, didn't he?"

Kelly sighed. She hadn't told him that because she hadn't wanted him to worry. "He said that it *might* be dangerous."

"And you weren't even going to tell me?"

"Okay, I should have told you, but you should have told me before you made a decision that affected both of us."

"I'm telling you now, and it's already done."

Pressing a finger against Hawke's lips to break the suction, Blade turned him and transferred his attention to her other breast. "I did it without telling you because you were still weak and I didn't want to upset you. You wouldn't have changed my mind anyway. It's not up for discussion. It's done, and you're not getting pregnant again. We're very lucky to have the child we have. No more, Kelly. You're everything to me, and I can't go through the nightmare of almost losing you again."

"I don't want to hear it's not up for discussion. I'm not done discussing it yet. How dare you make that kind of decision without talking to me about it first?" Kelly's stomach knotted as the distance between them became wider than ever.

Blade stiffened behind her. "I'll do whatever it takes to protect you."

Struggling to keep a relaxed hold on Hawke, Kelly gritted her teeth. "Blade, I'm so mad at you, I could scream. When the hell did you have this done?"

"A couple of weeks ago."

"Who went with you?" Kelly blinked back tears at the thought of him going through that without her at his side. "Apparently, you'd rather keep it a secret and go without me than telling me so that I could go with you."

Blade's hands tightened on her waist. "King took me, and I went to lie down at the club afterward."

"I should have been with you." She winced at the whine in her voice, but the hurt proved too strong to hide.

"You have enough to worry about. You're supposed to be resting, and Hawke needed you here."

Turning her head, she looked up at him over her shoulder. "I had the right to be there, Blade, and you know it. You should have talked to me about this before making a decision that affected both of us. I want more children."

Blade nuzzled her neck. "You've been through enough, both physically and emotionally. We have a beautiful, healthy son. It's a lot more than some people have. I'm just grateful every day to have both of you."

"Damn it, Blade, I'm grateful, too, but how would you feel if I went to have my tubes tied and didn't tell you about it until afterward?"

A pregnant silence followed, Blade tensing even more. "Fuck."

With a sigh, some of the tension left his body. "I would have understood that you were scared to get pregnant again, but I would have been very hurt—devastated—that you didn't talk to me about it. I get it, baby, and I'm sorry. I didn't mean to hurt you, I swear."

Burying his face against her neck, he sucked in a breath as though absorbing her scent. "My only excuse is that I was so damned scared of losing you. Terrified. I realize now that I should have talked to you. I just didn't want to worry you."

He brushed his lips over her shoulder in a loving gesture that warmed her all the way through. "I was wrong not to talk to you about it first. I didn't mean to hurt you, baby. I wouldn't hurt you for the world."

Tilting her head to give him better access, she moaned at the incredible feel of his lips and warm breath against her neck. "I'll forgive you if you promise to never keep anything from me again. I'm still mad because you did it behind my back." She'd been nervous about the possibility of getting pregnant again, but she wouldn't have told him.

Surprised at the sense of relief she felt, she took a deep breath and let it out slowly. "I want my husband back."

Gripping her chin, Blade turned her to face him, his eyes hooded. "You never lost me. I'm right here, and have no plans to go anywhere. You're stuck with me for life, my love."

"I want to make love again, the way we used to."

Blade smiled. "We used to make love in a lot of different ways. Was there anything wrong with any of them?"

Kelly narrowed her eyes, knowing damned well that he was backing her into a corner. "Of course not."

"There you go. As soon as my son goes back to sleep, I'm going to make love to you. I'm going to sink my cock into that sweet pussy and wring orgasm after orgasm out of you."

Just the thought of it made her stomach muscles tighten and her pussy spasm. "Yes. Oh, God, Blade. It's been so long."

Blade smiled and took Hawke, settling the sleeping baby against his bare shoulder. "Take that gown off. I want to reacquaint myself with that gorgeous body."

Eager to please him, and to make love again, Kelly worked the nightgown off and waited.

After settling Hawke in the bassinette, he rid himself of the towel and walked slowly back to the bed.

"Lie back. Arms above your head. Hold on to the headboard."

Kelly grinned, shivering at the steel and erotic intent in his voice. "God, I've missed this."

Standing over her, Blade fisted his cock. "Be quiet. Not a sound. Bend those legs and spread them."

Her breath caught at the demand in his voice, her body tightening at the heat in his dark eyes. Staring up at him, she bit her lip to hold back a moan as she bent her knees, flattening her feet on the mattress as she spread her thighs wide.

Staring down at her, Blade ran his fingertips up and down her inner thighs, making them tremble. "Not a sound."

Biting her lip to hold back a cry, and trembling even harder at the command in his low, whispered voice, Kelly nodded and tightened her grip on the headboard.

Her body burned under his heated gaze, every muscle quivering beneath the slow slide of his fingertips. Jolting when he tapped her inner thigh, Kelly obediently spread them even wider, her breathing becoming more ragged by the second.

Holding her gaze, Blade ran his fingertips over her bare mound before continuing upward. He ran them over her abdomen from side to side, moving higher with every pass. Bracing a hand on the mattress by the pillow, he leaned over her, watching her face as his fingers continued their upward journey.

Closing her eyes at the feel of his light touch skimming back and forth over the underside of her left breast, Kelly struggled to keep her trembling thighs parted against the rush of tingling heat that centered at her slit.

"Open those beautiful eyes."

Obeying him, Kelly lifted her gaze to his, her pulse tripping when he ran the tip of his finger over her nipple, digging her heels into the mattress at the sharp tingling in her clit. She needed to close her thighs against the ache that settled there, but she knew that Blade wouldn't allow it.

She knew her husband's moves well, and knew that if she closed her thighs, he'd purposely avoid giving her the attention she needed there.

It had been too long, and she wanted him too much to take the risk.

A fine sheen of perspiration coated her skin as he moved his attention from one nipple to the other, her ragged breathing the only sound in the room.

His dark eyes glittered hotly, flaring when she arched into his caress and bit her lip to hold back a cry.

"Very good, baby." The satisfaction in his faint smile and the pride and possessiveness in his nearly black eyes thrilled her, his entire demeanor and aura of power surrounding him sharper than it had been in months.

His fingers closed over her nipple, tightening just enough to create an intense pressure that bordered on pain, and sent another sharp tug to her clit and pussy. "Very good." He cupped her breast, massaging gently. "Did you think that just because I've been gentle with you that I've forgotten that all of this is mine?"

Sliding a hand down her body again, he parted her folds. "*All* of this is mine, and it's my responsibility to take good care of it. To take good care of *you*. I can caress you, spank you, whip you, or restrain you as I see fit. It's not up to you. It's up to me. Never forget that."

Kelly blinked back tears, the relief of having her dominant lover back so intense it nearly overwhelmed her. She opened her mouth to tell him, snapping it closed again when Blade's eyes narrowed and he shook his head.

Applying more pressure to her nipple, Blade leaned closer. "Not one fucking word." Staring into her eyes, he smiled when she bit her lip again to hold back her cry of pain and pleasure. "You want to tempt me? You want to dare me? You're going to have to accept the consequences. Understood?"

Nodding frantically, Kelly gulped in air, desperate to do as he demanded. Her gaze kept sliding to his cock, her pussy clenching at the evidence of his arousal.

Releasing her nipple, Blade straightened again. "Very good. Now pull those knees back to your chest."

Sucking in another deep breath, Kelly rushed to obey him, her movements clumsier than she would have liked due to her shaking.

The knowledge of what she felt shone in his eyes as he slid his hand down her body again. "Spread them wider, Kelly. You know better than that. That's it. Now, keep them there. Don't you dare lose your grip."

Kelly nodded again, knowing that he expected her to acknowledge everything he said to her even if he didn't permit her to speak, her breathing becoming shallow and more ragged as his hand continued lower. Her breath caught again at the slow trace of his fingers over her folds, the tingling in her clit becoming unbearable.

She fought to remain still—fought to remain silent—her toes curling with the effort it cost her. Every nerve ending in her body danced with the sexual awareness he'd created, the sizzling heat just below the surface screaming for his attention.

And he'd barely touched her.

Using her eyes to plead with him to end the torment, Kelly tightened her hold on the backs of her knees to keep her legs held wide the way he wanted.

The way he'd demanded.

She sucked in another breath when he pressed a knee to the mattress and settled between her spread thighs, shaking even harder.

Leaning back on one hand, he ran the backs of the other up and down her thigh, his gaze following the movement of his hand. "You're more beautiful than ever."

Kelly smiled and wiggled her hips, pleased that she'd lost so much weight.

Blade shook his head. "No, it doesn't have anything to do with the weight you've lost."

Kelly frowned, wanting to ask him what he was talking about, sucking in another breath when his fingers worked their way to her inner thigh, closer and closer to her slit.

"It's not your weight. It's your confidence." He tapped her clit, his eyes flaring when she sucked in a breath and stiffened. "Very good. I don't know if it's losing weight that's made you more confident, becoming a mother, or realizing exactly what you are to me—something you should have known long ago."

With a nonchalance that made his dominance over her even more pronounced, he circled the opening of her pussy with a firm finger, his gaze holding hers. "I'm delighted with your confidence, and think it's sexy as hell, but don't think for one minute that I won't demand submission from you."

Despite the hunger clawing at her, Kelly couldn't hold back a smile. A moan escaped when his finger plunged into her, a moan she swallowed almost immediately.

"Careful, love," Blade's voice held a hint of warning that made her pussy clench on his finger. "You've been pushing me for days. Did you think I would let you get away with that forever?"

Bending low, he brushed his lips over her mound, his eyes steady on hers as he moved his finger inside her pussy, pressing at a spot that he knew drove her wild. "You're my most valuable possession, love."

Smiling at her gasp, he raised a brow. "Indignant, are you? Well, too bad. You knew what you were getting into when you married me, and you've been pushing my limits to see how far you could go. This body is mine, and I'm taking care of it the way I see fit. You really have no say in it at all, so you'd better start behaving yourself."

He tapped her clit, his eyes narrowing when she jolted and gasped. "Keep absolutely still. No squirming. No jolting. Brace yourself, Kelly. I want to enjoy you and I don't want you moving around while I do it."

Knowing how good her husband was with that decadent mouth, Kelly sucked in another breath and nodded, squeezing her eyes closed as he lowered his head.

Blade moved his finger again, his slow strokes pressing against her inner walls. "Not a sound, and you stay exactly like this."

Her pussy clamped down on his finger, her clit throbbing at the feel of his warm breath caressing it.

Something about Blade seemed different, but with desire clouding her thoughts, she couldn't focus enough to figure out what.

Holding her breath, she waited, knowing just how potent and wicked her devious husband could be, but even after all the time she'd been married to him, she wasn't prepared for the intensity of his lips closing over her clit, nor for the strong tug as he sucked her clit *hard*.

Too aroused to hold back, she cried out at the sharp sensation, the tingling heat so extreme, she pushed her heels against the mattress to jerk away, groaning in frustration at the loss of contact.

Rushing to pull her knees back up again, she squeezed her eyes closed, her breath coming out in hoarse whimpers.

Hanging on the edge, Kelly fought the warning tingles, so close to coming that she wanted to scream. Frustrated that Blade let her get away, she waited with breathless anticipation for him to pull her back and put his mouth on her again.

And waited.

Trembling as the tingling grew stronger, the pleasure holding her on the razor sharp edge, Kelly whimpered in agony and looked down to see him braced on an elbow and watching her.

Gritting her teeth, she spread her thighs wider. "Please!"

Blade's cold smile sent a chill through her, one that did nothing to cool the heat raging through her. "It seems you've forgotten quite a bit, love. Or, did you think that I was going to be more lenient with you now?"

Stunned, Kelly could only stare at him as he rose from the bed to stand beside her.

She knew this Blade, and yet she didn't.

The Master she knew well lay somewhere behind Blade's dark, glittering eyes—the doting and overprotective husband apparent in the slight smile that played at his lips.

There was something, though, different about both of them— something she couldn't quite put her finger on—but that she wanted with every fiber of her being.

"Blade!" She couldn't stay silent, but she kept her voice at a whisper. "Please." Releasing her grip, she reached for him and started to rise. "I want—"

His smile fell, his expression hardening. "Did I tell you that you could move?"

Kelly stilled, searching his features, an erotic chill going through her at his warning beneath the deliberately casual question. "Um, no." She rolled to her back again, her face burning when Blade looked pointedly at her legs and back to her again, a dark brow going up.

Swallowing heavily, Kelly spread her knees and slowly lifted them to her chest, using her hands against the bottom of her inner thighs to keep them there. Taking a shuddering breath at the sharp awareness as Blade's heated gaze lingered on her slit, Kelly bit her lip to hold back another moan.

Blade moved to her side again and towered over her, running his hand up and down her shin, his expression hard and much colder. "You were told not to move, and you moved. You were told not to speak, and you spoke. You're obviously not as ready for this as you claimed."

She'd underestimated him.

It struck her suddenly how tender he'd been over the last year.

She'd almost forgotten the thrill that went through her when he looked at her with that gleam in his eyes.

Blade tapped her clit, his eyes narrowing when she stiffened and gasped. "Very good."

The mattress dipped as he knelt on it again and positioned himself between her thighs. "It appears you think I've gone soft."

Her gaze went to his cock, her mouth going dry even as her pussy leaked more moisture.

Blade smiled faintly. "No, not there. I'm always hard for you." Gripping the backs of her knees, he nodded toward the headboard. "Hold on to the headboard and don't let go."

Positioning his cock at her pussy entrance, he raised a brow. "Because you disobeyed me, you won't be coming tonight."

A whimper escaped before Kelly could prevent it. Tightening her hands on the slats of the headboard, she bit her lip to keep from begging him to let her come.

Hooking her legs over his arms, Blade braced himself over her with a hand pressed to the mattress on either side of her waist. "No coming tonight, love. You're going to pay for pushing me to do something you're not ready for."

* * * *

Blade had never been so close to losing control in his life.

Pressing his cock deeper into his wife's hot, velvety pussy, he watched her, unable to tear his gaze away.

The pink flush and sheen of perspiration made her skin look even softer and dewy, making him want to explore every beautiful inch of her.

She didn't speak, but mouthed *please* as he began to stroke in and out of her, her pussy clamping down on his cock with every slow thrust.

Keeping his tone cool and controlled cost him a great deal, but somehow he managed it. "I said no, Kelly. No coming. I won't let you."

The ripple of her inner walls around his cock warned him that she was close to coming, so he stopped stroking, forcing a cold smile. "Did you think I couldn't tell? I know your body, love, as intimately as I know my own."

His arms began to shake, his balls tight and hot as he waited for her to back from the edge, but he didn't allow his expression to falter.

She was so damned beautiful. So passionate. He knew he had to get control of the situation as soon as possible, and hope that dominating her in this way would put a stop to her need to challenge him, and convince her to let him take her with the tenderness she needed.

Once she settled some, he began thrusting into her again, alert to any change that would warn him that she was on the verge of coming.

Her soft cries tugged at his cock, and the knowledge of how easy it would be to send her over proved far too irresistible.

But, he had to resist.

He had to make sure that she stopped daring him to inflict the kind of erotic pain that she craved, but that she was far too delicate to accept now.

She was too damned delicate now, and it got harder and harder to resist her.

Blade sucked in a breath when she tightened on him again, so close to coming that his cock leaked moisture. "Again, love? You really need to come, don't you?"

Her soft, wet pussy sucked him in, the feel of her all around him stirring the Dominant inside him.

He pushed it back again, a task he found more difficult each time he did it.

He wanted her. Badly. He wanted to take her to the secret place that gave her the most pleasure, the place they'd discovered together.

He wanted her to come the way he knew she could, to have an orgasm so intense that she lost control of herself and let him take over completely.

Smiling at the fury and frustration that glittered in her eyes, Blade forced himself to remain still until she settled again, his patience and control stretched to the max.

The tingling in his balls couldn't be contained any longer and with several sharp thrusts in rapid succession, he let himself go with a groan, his entire body shaking with the force of his orgasm. The tingling travelled up and down his spine as he emptied himself into her, the force of his orgasm stunning him.

The need in Kelly's eyes ripped him to shreds, the desperate way she rocked her hips driving him insane.

With a curse, he withdrew, leaving his wife desperate and unsatisfied, something he'd never done to her before.

Gathering her close, he crooned to her, overcoming her struggles and running his hands up and down her back to calm her while trying to stop his own shaking. "Calm down, honey."

"I don't want to calm down, damn it! I want to come."

"No."

It was a word he didn't use often with her, and one that left a bad taste in his mouth.

It would be worth it, though, if the threat of being left unsatisfied curbed her daring.

He could only hope.

Keeping his voice hard and cold, he slapped her hand away from her clit, gritting his teeth against the need to make her come hard and fast over and over again until she was so weak, she forgot all about defying him.

"Please, Blade, don't do this to me." The tortured look in her eyes reminded him so much of the way she looked at him in the ambulance that he crumbled.

Damn it, he couldn't resist giving her whatever she wanted.

Holding on to his cold demeanor, he released her and stood next to the bed, determined not to give in to her completely.

"Fine. If you want to come, come. But, I won't help you."

He dropped down on to the bed again and waved a hand. "Be my guest."

He knew his wife well enough to be able to read her expression.

Her surprise that he would go back on his word and let her come mingled with a trace of disappointment.

Furious at himself for weakening, he crossed his arms over his chest and watched her, frowning. "Well? If you're going to masturbate, I want you to do it in front of me. Even though I'm not the one making you come, your orgasms still belong to me."

* * * *

Kelly blinked, not sure what had happened.

She was still aroused, but she didn't want to come at her own hand. She wanted to come at his.

"I'm not masturbating in front of you."

Blade's dark brow went up. "Then you're not masturbating at all."

Kelly gulped when he reached out to caress her nipple, the need to come still clawing at her. Not daring to move, fought the urge to press her thighs closed to release the throbbing of her clit.

"I'm sorry."

Blade's expression closed, his eyes becoming unreadable. "What are you sorry for?"

Suppressing her shrug, Kelly fisted her hands at her sides, the soft friction of Blade's finger over her beaded nipple sending sharp heat to her slit and making her tremble even harder. "For not obeying you. For pushing you."

Blade gave her nipple a last tap and stood, bending to pick up the towel before straightening to his full height. "Good. Remember that. I'll take you slow and easy until I feel that you're ready for more. Your insistence for me to give you more than you can handle isn't doing either one of us any good."

She blinked again as he strode back into the bathroom and closed the door behind him.

Still aroused, she got up from the bed and began pacing to work it off.

She couldn't leave things this way. She had to prove to her husband that she was strong enough to handle the dominant side of him—that she *needed* to submit to him again.

She wanted their sex life to get back to normal.

Pausing, she smiled to herself.

Their sex life had never been what she would have considered normal before she met him, but now the combination of tender loving, raw heated sex that burned up the sheets that sometimes included erotic pain and toys, and sessions in the playroom had become completely normal.

And she wanted it back.

Now, she just had to figure out how to goad Blade into doing it.

Without being left needy and frustrated.

* * * *

Bracing himself against the bathroom counter, Blade fought to get himself together.

He'd just had her and he wanted her again.

And again.

His hunger for her, stronger now than ever, made him even more determined to protect her from his own need to dominate.

He had to find a way to appease her need to submit, one that didn't stoke the fire of his need to dominate.

Now, he just had to figure out how to do it.

Without either one of them being left needy and frustrated.

Chapter Nine

Blade couldn't wait to get home to his wife.

He'd thought of little else all day, so distracted by thoughts of the way she'd been the night before that he'd missed an entire conversation that he and his business partners, Royce and King were supposed to be having.

He hadn't gotten a damned bit of work done, and had stared at the computer screen for an hour and a half, unable to focus on the application in front of him.

His darling wife was driving him crazy.

He'd lingered that morning, never tiring of watching her breast feed their son, and called her earlier just to hear her voice.

He'd thought he'd had it bad before, but after almost losing her, he didn't want to let her out of his sight.

He'd loved her almost from the beginning, but what he felt for her now was so much more.

It had been so long since he'd been able to make love to her the way that he knew they both needed, and the tension inside him made it difficult to focus on anything except her.

Tonight, he would make love to her with enough passion to satisfy both of them, but with the tenderness she deserved and needed.

King slapped him on the back, startling him out of his musings. "Why don't you go home? You're here, but your head's on your wife and son."

Blade scrubbed a hand over his face and reached for his coffee, hoping that some caffeine would help him focus. "No, I've already dumped too much on you and Royce." He took a sip of his coffee, grimacing to find it cold.

King grinned. "You're making more of a mess than you're helping. You've matched up submissives with other submissives, and booked two Doms into the same room at the hotel."

Grimacing, Blade pushed away from his desk. "To hell with it. I'll make it up to you when Brenna gets pregnant. Maybe by then, I'll have a handle on this." Turning his head, he looked at the monitor showing the empty playroom, and couldn't stop thinking about the first time he'd taken Kelly to his playroom and showed her the passion inside her, while teaching her to trust him.

They'd come a long way since then, and he'd loved every step of their journey.

King touched his arm. "You had a hell of a scare, and you and Kelly have been through a lot in the past year. You've been on pins and needles a long time. Things will settle back to normal soon, and when they do, you'll both feel better."

"Normal." Restless and edgy, Blade got to his feet and went to the window. "I don't know what the hell normal is anymore."

King chuckled. "You're probably sleep deprived. Once Hawke lets you get some sleep, you'll both feel better."

Hawke was a good sleeper, especially after eating so much before Kelly put him down for the night, but Blade nodded anyway. "You're right. I'll be at home if you need me."

"It's slow around here right now. I'll work on this for a while and then I'll go up to Brenna. Royce is already with her. Spend as much time as you can with Kelly and Hawke before this next group gets here."

"Yeah." Blade headed for the door, more anxious than ever to get to Kelly.

She'd been in a strange mood earlier, and he didn't like not knowing why.

Not knowing what his woman was thinking could be very dangerous.

* * * *

Careful to be quiet in case Hawke was sleeping, Blade entered his house, listening for Kelly as he hung up his coat and tugged off his boots. Hearing water running in the kitchen, he headed in that direction, his body tight with anticipation.

Finding his wife standing at the kitchen sink washing dishes, he paused at the doorway just to look at her.

The tight jeans she wore hugged her rounded bottom to perfection, making his hands itch to cup her there.

To yank her jeans down too her knees and press his lips against the soft, rounded flesh.

To turn her over his knee and spank her, warming her ass and spreading the heat until she squirmed over his lap and begged him to take her.

He had to be gentle with her now, but he sure as hell planned to hear those screams of pleasure again.

The playroom was soundproof.

No. He couldn't risk taking her there.

He'd have to keep her quiet so they didn't wake the baby and put an end to their loving.

"Where's Hawke?"

* * * *

Kelly cried out and jolted, startled by Blade's sharp tone. She'd been so deep in thought that she hadn't even heard him come in.

Turning at the waist, she smiled at the picture her husband made as he leaned against the doorway.

Blade looked at her much like he did when they'd first met—his eyes filled with hunger, and his body tight with tension.

Wiping her hands, she turned to face him, leaning back against the counter. "He's sleeping. You're home early. Is something wrong?"

Straightening, he strode toward her. "Yes, something's wrong. I can't get a damned bit of work done because I keep thinking about how much I want my wife."

Kelly grinned at his disgruntled tone, a jolt of lust going through her. Tossing the towel to the counter, she spread her arms wide. "She's right here. Oh!"

He gathered her against him, grabbing the baby monitor and attaching it to his pocket before lifting her high against his chest. He turned and strode from the room and to the stairs. "You're driving me crazy. I want you too damned much. I want to hear you come over and over and I want to sink my cock into you and feel you milk me."

Struck by not only his words, but the desperation and frustration in his tone, Kelly tightened her hands around his neck, pulling him down for a kiss, her entire body suffused in a wash of heat that settled in every erogenous zone.

"Yes. Damn, I've missed this."

Pausing on the steps, Blade pressed her against the wall and took her mouth in a searing kiss, growling in his throat when she tangled her tongue with his. Pulling back slightly, he nipped at her bottom lip just hard enough to make it sting. "Behave."

She knew that tone well, and her body responded instinctively to it, already anticipating the pleasure to come. Her nipples beaded tight against her bra, moisture already dampening her panties as her pussy prepared to accept him.

He lowered his mouth to hers again, kissing her with a possessiveness and firmness that established his dominance in a heartbeat, his hands tightening around her as he lifted his head and started up the stairs again.

"Every sweet inch of you belongs to me."

Kelly smiled, relief making her dizzy. "You made that pretty clear from the beginning, didn't you?"

"I hope so." His eyes narrowed. "Pleased with yourself, are you? Just remember, that we're doing this my way."

Running her hand over his chest, Kelly nodded solemnly, but couldn't quite hold back her grin. "Yes, sir."

Thrilled at the flash of heat in his eyes, Kelly ran the tips of her fingers through his hair, frowning when he paused next to the bed. "Aren't we going into the playroom?"

Blade always kept the door locked, and she hadn't been in the room since the night he'd packed everything away.

She wouldn't be happy until he had everything back in place again.

He set her on her feet and started stripping her out of her clothes, ripping the material of her shirt in his haste to undress her. "No."

Naked, Kelly reached for him, rubbing her nipples against his chest. "Oh, Blade. I want to use the playroom again. We can make as much noise as we want in there."

Lifting her again, Blade placed her on the bed, running his hand from her neck to her belly, leaving behind a trail of heat that made her nipples bead tighter and sent a rush of heat to her clit, making it throb. "I said *no*, Kelly. Do you really think I need a special room and toys to earn your submission?"

"Of course not." Watching him undress, Kelly shifted restlessly on the bed, trembling with need and anticipation.

He sounded so much like the dominant lover she knew so well that she found herself blinking back tears. His hurried movements and the sexual tension surrounding him spoke of his need for her, easing some of the fears still plaguing her.

Unable to look away from the sight of his cock, Kelly yelped when Blade gripped an arm and leg and flipped her to her belly.

Pressing a hand to her back, he bent to scrape his teeth over her shoulder in warning. "Quiet, or I'll gag you."

She shivered as he ran a hand over her bottom, a moan escaping when his fingertips pressed against her sensitive skin.

"Spread your thighs."

Rushing to obey him, Kelly spread her thighs several inches apart, crying out in surprised delight when Blade plunged a finger into her. "Oh, God, Blade. Yes."

Pumping her hips, she threw her head back and moaned, clamping down on his finger, and closed her thighs on his hand. "So good." She loved when he touched her like this, so possessively as if he owned her.

"What the hell do you think you're doing?" The disbelief and sharp edge of warning made her clit swell and coated his finger with another rush of moisture.

"I want you so much. Don't tease me, Blade. Just take me like you want me more than anything. Take me the way you used to."

Growling when Blade withdrew his finger, she waited expectantly for the slap to her bottom, but he rubbed her ass cheeks instead. "It looks like I'm going to have to gag you after all."

Shaking with excitement, Kelly watched Blade open the nightstand drawer and retrieve the ball gag he'd used on her several times in the past. Staring into his eyes, she drew a shaky breath at the intensity in his dark gaze, opening her mouth when he pressed the gag to her lips.

Shaking as he expertly fastened it, she stilled at the familiar, but almost forgotten sensation of her senses sharpening.

It was as if a switch turned on inside her, attuning her to Blade.

Even the slight change in his breathing as he finished fastening the gag alerted her that his mood had shifted, his need to dominate more intense. Her breath caught at the slow slide of his hand down her back, a loving caress screaming of ownership.

God, she'd missed this!

Another moan escaped, this one muffled by the gag, pinpricks of pleasure breaking out all over her skin at the brush of satiny material sliding up her legs, over her bottom and up her back.

"It's been a long time since I blindfolded you."

Unable to speak, Kelly nodded enthusiastically, delighted to have her Master back.

Fisting a hand in her hair, Blade bent low and turned her head to face him. "I wasn't asking permission, love." His eyes, dark and hooded, lingered on hers as he traced a finger over her lips, the silence lengthening.

Staring up at him and struck by the emotion in his eyes, Kelly hardly dared to breathe. Her lips tingled around the ball gag where he touched them, shivers of delight breaking out all over her body.

His caress softened on her lips, his eyes narrowing at her low whimper. Suddenly, he blinked as if coming out of a trance, and with a frown, followed by a slow smile, he slipped the fabric over her eyes and secured it. Running a hand over her bottom, Blade touched his lips to her shoulder. "You belong to me. Every gorgeous inch of you. Nothing in this world matters as much as knowing that you're mine."

Sliding a hand to her breast, he stroked a nipple, the firm confidence in his touch igniting her senses and creating a hunger that only he could satisfy.

"All mine."

His lips moved over her back, sending sharp tingling heat to her slit. "My greatest fantasy."

His fingers closed over her nipple as his lips moved lower. "My greatest joy."

Blindfolded, she had to rely on her other senses, and found herself more attuned to him than she'd been in a very long time.

Shivering with delight, she sucked in a breath when the mattress dipped and Blade spread her legs, making a place for himself between her ankles. Her pussy clenched at the rush of air over her slit, another moan escaping when he lifted a foot and touched his warm lips to her ankle.

Fisting her hands in the pillow, Kelly was glad that Blade had gagged her to muffle the hoarse moans that continued to pour out of her.

His lips moved higher to her shin, and then to the back of her knees, spreading her thighs wider as he moved forward. Running his lips up the backs of her thighs, he slid his fingers higher to caress her inner thighs. "You're always wet for me, aren't you, love?"

Desperate for friction against her throbbing clit, Kelly lifted her hips, and groaned, writhing to get closer to his fingers.

Blade moved his fingers away, thwarting her, and lifted her other ankle. "See, baby? Doesn't this feel good?"

God, yes!

Pressing her face into the pillow, she shivered at the feel of his lips moving higher, another ragged moan escaping when he scraped his teeth over the sensitive skin of her lower curve of her bottom cheek.

The heat at her slit drove her crazy, her pussy clenching with the need to feel him inside her. Her muscles quivered beneath the slow slide of his hands and lips, her body responding with joy at the tender ministrations of its Master.

She knew how she must look, rocking her hips and wagging her ass at him in a desperate attempt to get friction against her clit, but she was too far gone to care.

Her body came to life under his hands, every touch designed to give pleasure and increase her already raging hunger for him.

She threw her head back, another moan escaping when his hands closed over her buttocks. Her breath caught, and then came out in sharp pants as his thumbs began a slow journey down the crease of her ass.

Shivering, she lifted the pillow, pressing it against her mouth to muffle her cries as Blade parted her cheeks, exposing her bottom hole.

Groaning at the sharp awareness—the pinpricks of pleasure surrounding her puckered opening—Kelly squeezed the pillow tighter, her breath coming out in short, desperate pants.

Shaking with anticipation, she jolted when his tongue flicked out to touch her there, the erotic shock to her system forcing another cry from him.

Her delicate flesh burned, the heat spreading to her slit as another rush of moisture coated her inner thighs.

Knowing that one loud cry would wake Hawke and end everything, Kelly fought to be quiet, but her husband knew every inch of her body and used that knowledge to drive her to the brink of coming with a speed that left her breathless.

Crying out into the pillow again when he scraped his teeth over her bottom and moved up her body, she tilted her hips, rubbing her ass against his chest.

She arched her back as his hands slid under her to give him access to her breasts, her nipples aching for his attention, sucking in another sharp breath at the feel of his cock brushing against her thigh.

She wanted to beg him to take her—beg him to fuck her hard and deep—but the gag in her mouth made it impossible.

He knew.

Blade always seemed to be ten steps ahead of her in bed and knew what every touch would do to her. He knew how to make her move in a certain way and was always prepared for whatever she did.

She, though, could never anticipate him.

Instead of reaching for her breasts and giving her nipples the attention she needed, he reached for her hands, loosening her hold on the pillow and lacing his fingers with hers. Running his lips over her shoulder, he stretched her arms above her head as he slid his cock deep into her pussy, his thighs keeping hers held wide.

"Come for me, love."

Kelly had no choice. His slow, deep thrusts forced her to the edge and pushed her over, the friction of his hot, steely cock making it impossible to hold back. The hot waves washed over her, and throwing her head back, she turned her head to the side, crying out again at the scrape of his sharp teeth over her neck.

With another cry into the pillow, she clamped down on his cock, rocking her hips to try to get him to hurry his thrusts, but she already knew she could never hurry Blade.

Thrusting in a slow, steady rhythm, Blade tightened his hands on hers. "That's it. Yes. I love the feel of your soft pussy clamping down on me. Hmm. Very good, love. How about another?"

A shiver went through her at his tone.

She didn't bother to answer, knowing he didn't expect one.

It was his way of warning her that he would make her come again, and nothing she said or did would prevent it.

Already she could feel herself climbing again, the smooth thrusts of her husband's cock stretching her pussy walls, every bump and ridge of his cock providing a delicious friction.

His steely length forced her pussy to accommodate him, so hard and hot as he thrust deep inside her.

Transferring both of her hands to one of his, Blade nuzzled her neck. "All mine. Feel how your pussy grabs me. It knows who it belongs to, doesn't it, love? So does this clit."

Kelly bit down on the gag to hold back a cry as Blade slid a hand down her side, and paused just long enough to tug a sensitive nipple before slipping under her, raising her hips even higher as his fingers settled over her clit.

Oh, God!

Knowing how good Blade could be with those fingers, Kelly cried out and tried to buck, but Blade's weight held her in place.

She wanted it to last and she knew that he could make it linger, and torture her, or make her come so hard and fast. If he did that, he'd make her come again and again, her sensitive clit no match for the touch of its Master.

Chuckling softly, Blade moved his fingers with a speed that made her body tighten almost immediately, her juices easing the slide of them over her clit.

"You trying to get away from me, baby? You know I can't allow that. I told you what was going to happen to you. Come again, Kelly. Now."

No matter how many times he'd done this to her, or how hard she fought to resist coming at his command, she'd never been able to do it.

This time proved no different.

Her body responded to the velvet layered over steel, tightening as the pleasure in her clit exploded in a rush of heat. Pressing her face into the pillow again to hold back her cries, she fought to close her legs as the intensity became almost unbearable, but Blade's powerful thighs kept hers held wide.

"Good girl." His strokes to her clit slowed and softened, not stopping until the last waves of her orgasm washed over her. "Let's take you down nice and slow. That's it, baby."

He always knew.

She'd asked many times how he knew when she was about to come, and how he knew when the last waves rippled through her, but a slow smile had always been his only answer.

Stilling when he withdrew, she lifted her head again just as he rolled her to her back, and before she could suck in another breath, he jerked her to his lap and thrust into her again. Reaching up, he removed the blindfold and tossed it aside, staring into her eyes. "Look at you. I love when you get that glazed look in your eyes. You don't think you can come again, but I'm going to show you that you can."

He licked her lips around the ball gag. "I can make you."

Gripping his shoulders, Kelly gasped when the hand on her back tightened to hold her while his other cupped her breast and began to tug at her nipple.

His eyes, dark and hooded, held hers. "Do you have any idea how much pleasure it gives me to know that you're mine?" Lowering his head, he kissed her over the gag, nibbling at her lips as he readjusted his hold.

Sliding his hand to a spot between her shoulder blades, and the other to her bottom, he leaned her back and began to thrust into her again. "All of you. Isn't that right, Kelly?"

Staring into his eyes, Kelly struggled to hold back another cry at the feel of his finger sliding through her slick juices and to her puckered opening.

She knew what he would do. She saw it in his eyes just a second before he pressed his finger against her forbidden opening.

Digging her hands into the thick muscle of his shoulders, Kelly tightened, her toes curling at the effort it cost her to hold back another cry as he pushed his finger past the tight ring of muscle and into her.

Her position left her bottom open and unprotected, leaving her no way to prevent it.

She loved it that way, and her husband knew it.

Blade smiled as he slid his finger deep. "Your pussy and ass are clenching hard, aren't they, love? Poor baby needs to come again."

Shaking everywhere, her skin damp with perspiration, Kelly let her head fall back as Blade began thrusting again.

She didn't know how he did it, but he could take her from one orgasm to the next with no apparent effort. The feel of his finger moving in her ass with every thrust of his cock sent her soaring with no warning at all.

With one hand on her bottom and the other at the back of her neck, Blade moved her on his cock and finger, his eyes narrowing at her whimpered cry as she came again.

Thrusting hard and deep, he groaned and buried his cock deep inside her as he found his own release, his big body shaking as he emptied his seed into her.

Pulling her against his chest, he pressed his face into her hair, his breathing ragged. "There, baby. You're okay."

Releasing the ball gag, he urged her to sit up. "Open."

Kelly opened her mouth wider to allow him to take the gag, a whimper escaping when he moved the finger in her bottom again. "Blade."

"Yes, love?"

To her consternation, a sob escaped.

Withdrawing the finger from her ass, Blade placed her on the bed and loomed over her, his eyes frantic. "What's wrong? Did I hurt you?"

Shaking her head, Kelly blinked back tears and shook her head, reaching out to cup his jaw. "No. Of course not. I've just missed this so much. I was afraid that after having the baby, you didn't want me that way anymore."

Blade's expression softened. "I always want you."

Kelly laughed through her tears, careful to keep her voice low. "So you'll put everything back in the playroom again?"

Blade smiled and rose from the bed, bending to press a kiss to her nipple. "Everything's going to be fine, Kelly. You worry too much. I'll never stop wanting you."

Mesmerized by the sight of her husband's gorgeous ass as he walked away, Kelly didn't realize until he'd closed the door behind him that he hadn't answered her about the playroom.

Sitting up, she wrapped her arms around her knees and stared at the closed door, remembering the look in his eyes right after he'd come.

His eyes had been filled with love and glittering with satisfaction, but she'd learn to read him well enough to know that he'd held back.

Grinning, she shoved the covers aside and stood, stretching.

Her plan was coming along nicely.

Despite his formidable control, Blade's passions couldn't be held back forever.

She'd just have to push him.

Chapter Ten

She was driving him out of his mind.

Sitting forward at his desk, he glanced at Royce, who frowned in concentration as he matched Dominants with the submissives that had been accepted for the training classes.

Getting to his feet, Blade left the room and went into the hallway for more privacy, switching his cell phone to his other ear. "What did you say?"

"I said that I found everything in the attic. After I put Hawke down for his nap, I'm going to go up and bring it all down so I can set up the playroom again."

He clenched his hand, fisting it at his side, the need to turn her over his lap and paddle her ass making his palm itch.

"What the hell were you doing up in the attic?"

"Looking for toys, of course."

Gritting his teeth against the stirring in his groin, Blade injected a cold edge of command in his voice. "The attic is out of bounds for you. Stay out of there, and stay out of my things."

Her voice lowered. "But Blade, they're *our* things." Her giggle tightened his balls. "I want to play with them."

"No." In the past, just telling her no would have been enough, but he had a feeling that this time it wouldn't.

"I'm not sure how you had everything arranged before, so I'll just arrange them the way I want them."

She'd blithely ignored his command.

Ignored him!

His cock lengthened, pressing uncomfortably against his jeans. "You. Will. Not." Smiling, he reached into his pocket and pulled out his key ring, staring down at it. His smile fell, the blood rushing to his cock so fast it made him dizzy. "The key for the playroom was on my key ring, and now it's gone."

"Yeah. I took it and made a copy. You can have yours back when you get home."

Closing his eyes, he braced a hand on the wall, struggling for control. "What, exactly, do you think you're doing?"

"You're a smart man, Blade. You know exactly what I'm doing."

Blade jerked upright, his eyes flying open. "Kelly?"

She'd hung up on him!

"You okay?"

Blade looked up to find Royce scowling at him. "Yeah. Fine. Great."

Storming past him, he tossed his phone and keys onto his desk before he gave in to the urge to throw them against the wall. He dropped into his seat, only to bounce back up again. "She's driving me crazy. She knows how to push every fucking button. I'm a Dominant, damn it. I can control myself. A Dom without control is worthless, and my darling wife is stretching my control to the breaking point."

Royce closed the door and approached, propping himself on the corner of his desk. "Want to talk about it?"

"No." Blade paced to the window and looked out toward his house. "She's so damned delicate. Fragile."

Turning, he paced back the other way. "You saw her. You saw the way she looked. Pale and helpless."

Royce frowned. "She's okay, isn't she? I thought the doctor said that he was delighted by how well she was doing, and that she'd made a complete recovery."

"Yeah." Blade shifted his shoulders, hoping to relieve the tension there. "She went on a diet and has been exercising like crazy."

"Is she overdoing it?"

Blade snapped his head up and strode back to the window. "The doctor said she wasn't, but I think she is. She's been losing weight like crazy. Why the hell would she want to do that? I would think she would know by now that I wanted her like hell just the way she was."

Royce shrugged. "Brenna said she stopped in to see Kelly and Hawke the other day. Kelly was so happy with how the baby weight was coming off, that she wanted to see if she could lose a few more pounds, but she didn't want to lose the curves you loved so much. Brenna was concerned, but she said that Kelly checks with the doctor and promises that she's not going to go crazy with losing weight."

Smiling, Royce leaned back. "Seems Kelly has something she's trying to fit into—a surprise for you."

Blade turned and began pacing again. "I liked her the way she was. She didn't have to lose weight for me—but that's not even the worst part."

Scraping a hand through his hair, he turned again, meeting Royce's gaze. "Having a baby and losing weight has given her a confidence she never had before. She's constantly challenging me. Daring me to spank her. She wants to go back into the playroom again, for God's sake!"

Frowning again, Royce shook his head. "What's wrong with that?"

Whirling from the window, Blade glared at Royce, wondering if his friend had lost his mind. "Are you crazy? I dismantled the whole fucking thing when I brought her home. You can't possibly think I'd ever take her back in there after what she'd been through!"

Closing his eyes, Royce scrubbed a hand over his face. "Oh, hell, Blade. No wonder Kelly's so determined to lose weight and is doing things to temp you. You're not treating her the way you did before."

Blade gaped at him. "She just had a baby! She was in a fucking coma! You were there. You saw her."

Royce nodded. "And I saw your reaction. You're scared. That's understandable." Shaking his head, he sighed. "I can only imagine what that felt like. King and I have put off trying to get Brenna pregnant because Kelly scared us so much. I don't know what we'd do if we had to go through that with Brenna."

Blade nodded, relieved that someone else understood. "Exactly." Blowing out a breath, he began pacing again. "Kelly doesn't see it that way, though. I'm trying to appease her, but it's not working. Christ, the last thing I want to do is hurt her."

"I understand the position you're in, but it sounds like she wants to get back to the way things were before. She's insecure about your relationship. I'm sure she's afraid that you won't see her the same way again, and she needs that. She needs *you*."

With a sigh, Blade dropped back into his chair, his stomach in knots. "I know all about a woman's need to feel desirable. She should know how much I want her. I can barely keep my hands off of her. I realize that after having a baby, and the problems she had that kept us from making love for months that she'd need to feel better about herself."

With a furious swipe of his hand, he sent the papers on his desk flying. "Fuck!" He jumped to his feet again. "I love her more than my own fucking life! I'd do anything for her."

Blowing out a breath, he reached for the control that Kelly had all but shattered, and went to the window again, looking in the direction of the house he'd built for her. From this angle, he could see part of the roof, and knew that if he didn't get home within the next hour, she'd be climbing back into the attic. "I couldn't live with myself if I hurt her."

"And you won't." Getting to his feet again, Royce laid a hand on Blade's shoulder. "You know that. I know that, and more importantly, Kelly knows that. Neither one of you will be happy if you hold back. Go to her, Blade. Go to your wife and give her what you both need."

With a smile, he went to Blade's desk and tossed his keys and phone to him. "I won't expect you back today."

* * * *

Kelly bent to kiss Hawke's head. "Are you sure, Jesse?"

Jesse cooed at the kicking baby in her arms. "Are you kidding? I'm looking forward to this very much." Glancing up at Kelly through her lashes, Jesse grinned. "I'm probably not supposed to tell you this, but Clay and Rio have already started training a horse for Hawke. They're impatient to teach him to ride."

Giggling, Kelly finished packing the bottles of breast milk. "I think he's a little young for that."

"Yeah, but they want to be ready." Shifting Hawke to her shoulder, Jesse accepted the overnight bag. "I think they have plans to spoil Hawke rotten." Jesse grinned impishly. "So do I. Have fun with Blade tonight and don't worry about Hawke. Clay and Rio will probably have him watching a Western tonight and explaining everything to him."

Holding the door open for her best friend, she dropped another kiss on Hawke's head. "Jesse, thank you so much."

"You're welcome." Turning on the front steps, Jesse grinned. "Go put that sexy thing on. If I know Blade, he'll be pulling into the driveway any minute."

A shiver of anticipation washed over Kelly as she looked down the street toward the club. "I'm counting on it."

Chapter Eleven

Kelly pressed a hand to her stomach and turned again to look at herself in the mirror. She'd shopped at Logan's Leathers and bought something guaranteed to get Blade's attention.

The form-fitting leather hugged her curves, the strategic cutouts leaving her breasts, bottom, and slit exposed.

She couldn't wait to see Blade's reaction to the sight of her in the one-piece suit of buttery leather, smiling as she pulled her hair into a ponytail to keep it out of the way. The action lifted her breasts, and gave her the opportunity to see what she would look like if Blade fastened her hands above her head.

He might, especially when he learned that she'd finished setting up the playroom days ago.

She slipped on the leather boots that she needed for height, and that, along with the whip that Blade had used on her countless times, would complete her look.

Snapping the whip against her palm, she winced, shaking her hand against the sharp sting.

Damn, she'd have to be careful with that. How the hell did Blade make it make that sound without hurting that much?

Throwing it on the counter, she checked herself in the mirror again, grimacing when she saw that she'd chewed most of her lipstick off. After smoothing on another coat of "Passion Red," Kelly tossed the tube back onto the counter, stilling at the sound of a car door closing.

Blade was home!

She ran halfway to the playroom when she realized she'd forgotten the whip.

She ran back, grabbed the whip, and just made it to the playroom when the front door opened. Struggling to slow her breathing, she tightened her sweaty palm on the whip.

And waited.

* * * *

Storming into the house, Blade paused to close the door quietly behind him, not wanting to wake Hawke.

He didn't want any interruptions, not even from his beloved son, while he dealt with his darling wife.

Not hearing anything, he shrugged off his leather jacket, hanging it in the closet before going in search of Kelly.

Climbing the stairs, he listened for any sign of movement, but heard nothing.

She was home, though. He felt her.

He went first to the attic access, relieved to find it still closed.

Pleased that he'd gotten there in time, and assuming that the absolute silence meant that Kelly must be feeding Hawke, he went down the hall to their bedroom, pausing at the doorway.

Frowning to find it empty, he went to the bassinette, surprised to find it empty, too.

He turned away with the intention of searching the rest of the house, his gaze automatically going to the door to his playroom. Seeing the door partially open, he came to an abrupt halt, every muscle in his body tightening with anticipation.

Hunger.

His cock stirred, his blood boiling with the need to earn his wife's submission.

With slow stealth, he crossed the room, listening for any sounds that would give him a clue to what she was doing.

Hearing nothing, he paused at the doorway, pressing a hand against the heavy steel door to open it wider.

Expecting to find Kelly rummaging through boxes and putting items away in the cabinets, he froze in stunned stupefaction at the sight that greeted him.

He almost swallowed his tongue.

Careful to keep his expression hard and cold, he gritted his teeth and allowed his gaze to rake over her.

Standing in front of the leather table that he'd dismantled and stored in the attic, his wife apparently waited, slapping a whip against her palm. Her arms, breasts, and slit were exposed and framed by the leather that covered every other delectable inch of her.

Her red lips curved in a smile that could only be construed as devious.

"Hello, Blade. I've been expecting you."

Afraid that his voice would give away the sexual tension as the Dom inside him roared to life, he had to swallow heavily before speaking. Keeping his voice as cold and calm as possible, he stepped into the room and closed the door behind him. "So I see. Would you care to tell me what you think you're doing?"

His hands itched to cup her breasts, his palms tingling with the need to feel her beaded nipples press into them.

Her bare mound glistened with the moisturizer she used, and the knowledge of how soft and smooth she would be made his cock throb even harder.

Seeing her in leather, and by the sight of the soft, dewy skin revealed by the cutouts, it took every ounce of self-control Blade possessed to remain in place. Planting his feet, he crossed his arms over his chest and raised a brow expectantly.

Apparently not realizing the tight rein he held on his control, Kelly sauntered toward him, tapping the soft whip he'd used on her many times against her palm. "Waiting for you, of course."

His cock throbbed unbearably, so hard that he expected it to break through the zipper of his jeans at any moment. His entire body shook with need for her, the Dominant inside him demanding her submission.

Her surrender to whatever he wanted from her.

"Where's Hawke?"

Kelly smiled and licked her lips, making his balls tighten. "He's spending the night with Jesse."

The knowledge that he had her all to himself for the night forced a bead of moisture from his cock and made his balls so tight, they ached.

Imagining her on her knees before him, her painted lips wrapped around his cock, Blade forced himself to remain still as she circled him. "You've broken several rules, haven't you, love?"

Kelly had the audacity to run the whip over his back, something she would pay for in spades. "I don't think the rules apply any longer, now do they?"

Recognizing the trap she baited for him, Blade nevertheless allowed her to lead him in, confident that he would have the upper hand before they left the room.

He waited until she came around him again, holding her gaze. "Why would you think that?"

Moving to stand directly in front of him, Kelly began to unbutton his shirt. "Since you no longer dominate me, those rules are no longer in effect. As a matter of fact, I think it's time for me to lay down my own rules."

Forcing himself to remain still while she unbuttoned his shirt and ran the tip of the whip over his chest, Blade fisted his hands at his sides. "Excuse me?"

"You heard me." The sound of his shirt ripping was like pouring gasoline on a flame. As she pushed the edges of it aside, Blade came to the realization that this could only end one way.

Only years of practice, and the knowledge that he was only allowing her to dig a bigger hole for herself kept him from reaching for her.

Tracing the tip of the whip over one of his nipples, Kelly grinned up at him, her eyes alight with challenge.

"You've been a bad boy. You got a vasectomy without talking to me first." Narrowing her eyes, she reached out to cup his cock. "This cock is mine. You have to have my permission to do anything like that."

Blade allowed a small smile, anger causing a chink in his control. "Your doctor told me that getting pregnant again would be dangerous for you." Pleased with her look of uncertainty, Blade took a step forward, the Dominant inside him delighting when she took a nervous step back. "You didn't tell me that, did you, love? Did you really think I would do anything to endanger your health or safety by selfishly demanding that you give me another child?"

Kelly's eyes lowered, pleasing him immensely. "Well, no. That's why I didn't tell you. We wanted at least two."

"I want my wife. I won't risk having another child. Not even for you."

She lifted her chin, making his cock jump. "Okay. You're right. I have to admit it's a relief not to have to worry about it anymore. I wanted more children, but I want to be with you more."

"Good. Then that's settled." He started forward, only to have Kelly slap a hand to his chest.

Her infractions, especially while in the playroom, kept piling up.

"Wait." She dug a short nail into his chest, her eyes flashing. "That doesn't excuse the rest. Just because I can't have more children doesn't mean that I'm too fragile to have a sex life."

Blade raised a brow at that, delaying the inevitable. "You have a sex life."

"I don't have the sex life I had before, and neither do you. So, I've made a decision."

The knots in Blade's stomach turned to ice. "What kind of decision?" His tone, just as icy, made Kelly's eyes widen in alarm, and she turned away, affording him a view of her leather-framed ass.

Inwardly smiling at the plans he had for that ass tonight, he watched her hips sway as she walked away,

"Well, since you don't plan to dominate me—" Spinning, she tapped the whip against her hand again, her eyes now full of challenge. "I've decided that I'll just have to dominate you." Her words and her saucy smile had the Dominant inside him clamoring to get free.

Adding insult to injury, she reached out with the whip, tapping the bulge at the front of his jeans and making his cock jump again. "You're going to submit to me. Now, be a good boy and stand over here. I want you to raise your arms so I can attach those cuffs."

She pointed to the cuffs hanging down from the ceiling, one elegant brow going up. "I'm waiting."

With the challenge still ringing in his ears, Blade smiled coldly as the Dominant inside him broke free.

He reached her in two strides.

* * * *

Kelly had counted on a reaction from Blade, but the one she got turned out to be more than she'd bargained for.

He leapt toward her, and before she could even take a step back, he gathered her around the waist, lifting her off the floor and yanked the whip from her grip. With a slow smile, Blade tossed the whip aside and lifted her to sit on the leather table.

"I know how sensitive those nipples are. It wouldn't take much at all to have you writhing on the table, would it, baby?"

The hunger glittering in his hooded eyes was one she recognized well.

Thrilled with his reaction, Kelly let her gaze lower to his sensuous lips. "What do you think of my outfit?"

He ran a hand over her breast, pushing her hands lower to make her breasts thrust out even more. "I think you like looking for trouble."

Her breath caught at the friction of his palm against her nipple, and she found herself rocking her hips at the answering pull to her clit. "Have I found it?"

Closing his fingers on her nipple, he applied just enough pressure to send a combination of pleasure and pain raging through her system. Her pussy clenched as need gripped her by the throat.

With little apparent effort, and a speed that never failed to stun her, Blade had her fastened to the leather table, her hands tied securely above her head to the other end. Standing between her thighs, he forced them wide and attached them to either side of the table, leaving her breasts and slit unprotected.

Looking down, she saw that he held the whip, tapping it against his hand the way she had, the aura of power surrounding him, much sharper than it had been in months. "Very nice. Very pretty." He ran the tip of the small leather whip over her clit, smiling faintly when she jolted.

Before she could suck in a breath, he brought the small, flat strip of leather down on her clit.

The heat stunned her, as it always did, the sharp pain becoming pleasure almost as soon as the pain registered. Crying out his name, she writhed on the table, but her bonds held securely, making it impossible to close her legs against the too-extreme sensation. "God, Blade, it's too much."

Tapping her clit lightly with the whip, he smiled faintly as he watched her squirm and had to raise his voice to be heard over her cries. "Been a while, hasn't it, Kelly? You didn't want to wait and work back up to this again. You had to push me, didn't you?"

"Yes!" Her stomach muscles tightened, the taps to her clit sending delicious warning tingles all through her slit. It felt so good—like a firm caress, and she was too hungry for him to hold back.

Lifting the whip, he brought it down on her mound, just hard enough to sting. "You really didn't think I was going to let you get off that easy, did you?"

Turning his back on her, he opened one cabinet after the other. "You've made a mess of this. I'm going to have to spend an entire day sorting and cleaning these."

Grabbing several items, he went to the small sink in the corner and began to wash several items—items that he obviously planned to use on her now. "I already washed everything with that cleanser you had packed."

Blade turned his head and turned the water off. "Did you?" Straightening, he began drying something that he kept hidden. "You're not allowed in this room unless I bring you in here. I've made that clear to you, haven't I?"

Squirming restlessly, Kelly smiled at the bulge in his jeans as he moved toward her again. "Yep. I was bad."

Pursing his lips, Blade nodded once. "And you know that when you're in this room, you're not permitted to touch me unless I tell you to, correct?"

Grinning, Kelly shifted restlessly as his heated gaze lingered on her breasts. "Absolutely. Sure you don't want me to dominate you?"

Thrilled with the flash of warning in his narrowed gaze, Kelly raised a brow, questioningly.

Blade ran his tongue over his teeth, giving Kelly the impression he was struggling not to smile. "I have never, nor will I ever be dominated."

Placing a hand on her belly, he unlatched something on the table that allowed him to lift her legs high and wide and with a click, locked them there.

"You, on the other hand, *will* submit to me, and you'll apologize for going up into the attic and getting these things without my permission."

"I did it for a good reason."

Blade brought the whip down on her clit, raising his voice to be heard over her shocked cry. "For stealing my keys."

Holding her breath when Blade tapped her nipple with the whip, Kelly started shaking. "I had to take your keys to put my plan in action. I was afraid you would figure out I took them the next day." Grinning, she moved her hips as much as her bonds would allow, shocked to find that her bottom hung slightly off the edge, something that she knew meant Blade had plans for her ass. "You have to admit, it got your attention."

"That's what you wanted, isn't it? My attention. Well, you're going to get it. You're also going to apologize for coming into this room without my permission, and for touching me without being told to."

"I like touching you, and how the hell was I supposed to get the room ready without coming in here?"

* * * *

Blade looked down at his belligerent wife and knew that he'd never seen anything as beautiful and exciting as Kelly dressed in leather, the challenge in her eyes daring him to force her to submit.

Seeing her this way had his cock leaking moisture, and he knew that to teach her a lesson, and give her what they both needed, he'd have to deny her orgasm until she became a quivering mass of need.

Only then would he force her to apologize, which she would resist for as long as possible, and when she gave in, he would know it was because she couldn't hold out any longer.

Then, he'd make her come over and over until she couldn't even think anymore.

Just thinking about it made his cock ache.

Reaching behind him, he retrieved the small vibrator that he'd already taken out, one that he attached to her with leather straps that he circled around her waist and thighs to hold it in place. Carrying the control for it with him, he smiled at the picture she made, trying to squirm on the table.

"Having trouble being still, aren't you, my little sub?"

He smiled at her glare, secure in the knowledge that even though she always objected to being referred to as his sub, the reminder of her position excited her.

Smiling, he tapped the button for the vibrator, her soft cry like a stroke to his cock. He planned to torment her quite a bit in the next several minutes, keeping her arousal at a fever pitch. "Go ahead and cry out. Only I can hear you, and after what you've put me through, I'm very much looking forward to your cries. You'll be cursing at me soon, and you'll pay for that as well."

Reaching over her, he smiled and licked her nipple as he unfastened her wrist and brought it down to fasten it to the hook on the outer edge of the table by her hip. "You taste delicious." He gently massaged her breasts, smiling at her soft moan of pleasure. "So soft and firm. You almost make it impossible for me to hold back."

"Almost?"

Unfastening her other wrist, he brought it to his lips before fastening it to her other side. "I wouldn't be much of a Dom if I couldn't control myself or my wife, now would I?"

After securing her wrists, he closed his fingers around her nipples, rolling them gently between his thumbs and forefingers, his heart swelling at the look of love and trust in her eyes.

"We do this my way." Bending until his nose almost touched hers, Blade smiled faintly. "You've always trusted me to give you want you need, and not more than anything you can handle. I need that trust from you, Kelly. I don't want you to try to push me into things you can't handle right now. Can you even imagine having clips attached to your sensitive nipples?"

Shaking his head at her frown, he brushed his lips against hers, reveling at their softness, a softness that would close over his cock very soon. "That doesn't mean I'm disappointed. You're everything to me, Kelly. I love everything about you, and you give me more satisfaction by smiling at me over the breakfast table than anything I've ever done in the past."

Pleased to see the relief in her eyes, he smiled and tapped her nipples. "Will you trust me?"

The tears in her eyes humbled him. "Always." Smiling, she managed to wiggle just enough to make her breasts sway. "But, you're not going to let this opportunity to have your way with me slip by, are you? After all, I spent a lot of your money on my fancy outfit."

Running a hand over her breast, Blade grinned and straightened. "Well worth every penny, my little sub." He tapped the button again, sending a gentle vibration to her clit, releasing the button almost immediately, his cock pounding furiously at her cry of pleasure. "But you've gotten yourself into quite a bit of trouble."

His cock jumped again when she pouted, but her eyes flashed with excitement. Seeing her struggle to move enflamed him, especially since he'd long ago learned just how aroused his wife got when she couldn't move and was forced to accept whatever he gave her.

Watching him as he ran his hands over her while moving to stand between her widely splayed legs, she sucked in another breath, and he couldn't help but notice that her trembling had increased. "A woman has to do what a woman has to do."

Running his fingers through her wet folds, Blade stared down at her slit, lifting the small vibrator out of the way. With her legs lifted and spread wide, her pussy, clit, and puckered opening were all visible—and vulnerable.

Placing the vibrator back in place, he tapped the button again, determined to keep her clit swollen and throbbing. Meeting her eyes again, Blade smiled coldly. "And a man has to do what a man has to do. It's been a long time since I've fucked your ass, Sub."

Just the thought of sinking deep into his wife's hot, snug ass nearly made him come on the spot.

He was too hungry for her, and knew he'd have to get some semblance of control back to prolong her torture for as long as possible.

"Yes, it has." Her moan sounded a little more ragged than before, her thighs shaking as another rush of moisture escaped to glisten on her bottom hole. "Think you can handle it?"

Christ, she excited him.

Reaching behind him, he grabbed the tube of thick lube. "Oh, I know I can handle it. I'm looking forward to sinking my cock into your tight ass and fucking some of the sass out of you."

He had no intention of ridding her of any of that sassiness he loved so much, especially since it had taken months to earn her trust after her relationship with an abusive boyfriend.

It had taken a long time, but they'd made the journey together, a journey that brought them closer every step of the way.

Now, she was a part of him.

Obviously secure in the knowledge that he would never hurt her, she wrinkled her nose at him. "Not a chance. Oh, God, Blade!"

His chest swelled at her cry, his gaze on hers as he sunk a heavily lubed finger into her tight ass. "The question is, my love, do you think *you* can handle it?" Pressing against her inner walls, Blade smiled at the way the quivering muscles tightened on his finger. "You've been a bad girl, and you know you're going to have to pay for that."

His cock jumped in excitement at her soft cry of hunger.

* * * *

Kelly shivered as Blade slid his finger free, her bottom clenching for more attention. She loved when he spoke to her with a slight growl in his silky tone, a playful tone layered over hard, cold steel.

Recognizing the tone as one he used when his control hung by a thread, she bit back a moan as he turned to retrieve another item from the cabinet. "I had to be bad to get your attention. Oh, God!"

No amount of struggling or pushing against the leather covered extensions he'd attached to her legs allowed her to move so much as an inch, and prevented her from moving away from the thick dildo he pressed against her puckered opening.

Blade watched her steadily, his eyes glittering with possessiveness and erotic intent. "Can't move away, can you, sub? Look how nice and exposed you are. Your pussy and ass are just begging for attention, aren't they? This rubber cock should fill your ass nicely until I take it out and fuck you there."

Kelly couldn't hold back a cry as Blade pressed steadily, forcing the tight ring of muscle to give way. She fisted her hands at her sides, panting as he pushed the hard rubber deeper.

"Blade, it burns."

Rubbing a hand over her leather-covered abdomen, Blade continued to watch her, his gaze sharp. "It's been a long time since your ass has been filled. Perhaps you should have thought about that before being so naughty. Yeah, that's it."

Secure in the knowledge that her husband watched closely to make sure she could keep up, Kelly tugged at her bonds, even more excited that they held firm. Crying out as he pushed the cock deeper, she tried to rock her hips against the vibrator covering her clit, hoping that he would turn it on again and send her over.

The throbbing in her clit grew stronger, threatening her sanity. She needed friction there, and needed him to take her, but Blade didn't appear to want to let her come anytime soon.

Chills of excitement and sensation raced up and down her spine as her husband continued to fill her ass, her pussy clenching hard and releasing more of her juices. "Blade, oh God. I need to come. I can't wait." Her ass burned around the rubber cock, her inhibitions disappearing more with every inch he gained.

Blade pushed the flat, soft plastic vibrator aside, exposing her clit. "You're going to *have* to wait." He withdrew the cock slightly, only to push it deeper. "I expect several apologies and a change in attitude before you do."

Teasing them both, Kelly shook her head, swallowing another cry of pleasure as he pushed the dildo deep and slid a finger over her clit. "Not a chance."

The pleasure was incredible!

Her clit felt so swollen and achy, the need for friction against it driving her wild. Squeezing her eyes closed, she threw her head back trembling and clenching on the hard rubber filling her ass. "Blade, touch my clit. Touch my clit. Touch my clit. Please. Pleasepleaseplease. Hurryhurry."

The snap of the whip on her swollen clit shocked her, the sting making her jolt. "No. Blade. Oh, God!"

Ripples of pleasure raced through her, the tingling heat of an orgasm, but not giving her the relief of one. Fighting the bonds on her wrists in a desperate attempt to cover her clit proved useless, her inability to get free exciting her even more. "Damn it, Blade. I should have known you'd make me suffer. Let me come, please! I'll be good from now on, I swear!"

Blade's soft chuckle washed over her. Moving from between her thighs, he wiped his hands on a towel before coming to her side, smoothing a hand over her breasts as he walked past. Positioning himself above her head, he tugged at her nipples. "You're such a liar, my little sub. You'll only be good until the next time you want to be punished."

His smile sent a shiver of excitement through her as he unlocked the part of the table her head rested on, and lowered it several inches, clicking it in place again. "You like your punishments too much, don't you, baby? You don't fear anything now, do you?"

Her breath caught as he unfastened his jeans. "I trust you. I know you won't hurt me, which is what I've been trying to tell you." Wishing she could reach out and touch him, she smiled when he freed his cock and started to throw off the rest of his clothing, her ass clenching on the rubber cock. "Take me."

After throwing the last of his clothing aside, Blade moved to stand over her. "First, I'm going to take that mouth. You know damned well what it does to me when you wear that lipstick."

Kelly smiled as she stuck out her tongue to trace the underside of his cock. Slightly disoriented with her head tilted back, she jolted at the feel of his hands sliding over her breasts. "I know. It's been a long time since I tasted you."

Thrilling at his groan, she obediently opened her mouth wide when he pushed the head of his cock against her lips, moaning at the exotic taste of her lover.

Blade's slow, shallow thrusts took him deeper, almost to the back of her throat. "Every time I see those lips painted red, I want to fuck your hot mouth, and you know it. You've got me all figured out, don't you, love? Well, I've got you all figured out, too. You knew that your defiance and that outfit would have me clinging to my control. You still think you're going to manage to make me lose it, but I've got news for you, baby. I'm not done tormenting you yet. I'm going to come, but you're not—at least not until you've suffered for pushing me."

Sucking him harder as the pleasure built, she groaned in frustration when he tugged her nipples and moved his hands away from her breasts. Writhing to get his attention back to them, she stilled, her entire body going stiff at the soft vibration against her clit.

Yes. So good.

Oh, God, she was going to come!

She sucked harder, her entire body trembling as she clamped down on the dildo in her ass, the warm fullness sending her racing toward the edge.

Suddenly, the vibrations stopped.

"Not yet, love. You're not coming until I whip that clit."

Growling in frustration, she twisted restlessly, sucking harder as Blade groaned and came. Delighted that she'd given him pleasure, but too aroused to be patient, she swallowed and sucked him harder, fighting her bonds and rocking her hips to get any friction she could.

Still stroking shallowly into her mouth, Blade massaged her breasts, tugging lightly at her nipples. "Now that you've taken the edge off, I can take my time with your punishment."

The smooth silkiness in Blade's voice sent both a thrill and chill of foreboding through her, the knowledge that her Master's patience had been restored and that he intended to make her accept his erotic punishment for her daring making her shake even harder.

Slipping his cock free of her mouth, Blade readjusted the table beneath her head again, lifting her to a reclining position, a position he used when he wanted her to see her own punishment.

Still standing behind her, he massaged her breasts. "You okay, baby?"

Smiling, Kelly looked up at him. "I'm fine, except for being aroused. You drive me crazy when you do this, but I have a feeling you know that."

Kissing her hair, Blade smiled and tugged lightly at her nipples. "Do what, love?"

Closing her eyes, she pressed her thighs against the leather, rocking her hips against the sharp pull of pleasure from his manipulation of her sensitive nipples. "You get me close to coming, and then pull me back, knowing damned well that as soon as you touch me again, I get more aroused."

"Hmm." Blade slid his hands to her shoulders and massaged gently. "That sounds downright diabolical." He came around to her side, grinning as he bent to touch his lips to a nipple. "It also gives me the chance to cuddle you a little when you need to settle." Lifting his head, he pushed her hair back, his eyes dancing with amusement and anticipation. "I think you've settled enough for now."

Holding the control for the vibrator in front of her, he held his finger over the button. "Let's wake that clit up again before it gets a taste of the whip."

Holding her breath, Kelly watched him push the button, a hoarse cry escaping at the gentle vibration against her clit. "Blade! Yes. More. More. Oh, God. Incredible. So good. So good." As the vibrations went through her, she couldn't help clamping down on the slippery dildo, a surge of alarm going through her when she felt it slipping out of her.

"Blade!" Just as she was about to come again, he turned the vibrator off, leaving her clinging to the edge and rocking her hips in a desperate attempt to get the friction she needed. "Son of a bitch! Blade, please!" She shivered again as the dildo slipped out of her ass, the sound of it hitting the floor earning her a frown from Blade.

"Weren't you supposed to keep that inside you?"

Her bottom and pussy both clenched at emptiness, her arousal so intense she snapped at him, throwing her head back and gritting her teeth as she struggled for control. "You used too much lube and made it slippery. How the hell am I supposed to—"

The sharp sting of the whip against her inner thigh cut her off, the shock of it more intense than the pain.

"Careful, sub."

Her gaze flew to his, and then to the whip, and then to his again, not trusting the look in his eyes, a look she knew well, and one she'd learned to respect. "Sorry. I couldn't keep it in."

"You should be sorry." Moving to stand between her thighs, he looked down at the floor pointedly. "You know better. It seems you've forgotten quite a bit over the last several months."

Squirming as he removed the vibrator, Kelly forced a smile, while inside she trembled at the thought of the whip on her tender and swollen clit. "I haven't forgotten a thing, but if I did, it's your fault. Did you plan to coddle me forever?"

"Yes."

Blade smiled and smoothed the flat piece of leather over her mound. "I did. But that's not what you need from me, is it?"

Sucking in a breath when the tip of the small whip moved lower, and slid back and forth over her clit, Kelly stiffened. "I need to be what you need, just like you need to be what I need. I need the connection we have when we're like this—like we're a part of each other. Oh, God, Blade."

He tapped the whip over her pussy, short light taps that heated, but didn't hurt. He'd done it to her a few times before when he'd been in his especially dominant mood, and she knew that before he finished, her entire slit would be tingling with heat and the slightest touch would drive her wild.

"I know what you need, baby." His short taps to her clit threated to send her over, the last one sharper than the others, and making her clit sting. He paused to roll on a condom, his heated gaze moving over her slit as he reached for the whip again.

The next one landed on her bottom hole, the unexpected sting reawakening the awareness there.

He continued, short taps that warmed and awakened every nerve ending, intermingled with sharper snaps of the whip that stung enough to sharpen the sensation there, but not enough to cause any pain.

Blade knew her well, and knew how to hold her on the verge of coming without letting her go over.

It drove her mad!

With her eyes closed, she threw her head back, writhing as much as her bonds allowed as the sensations layered over each other and she knew nothing but hunger.

And Blade.

Light taps to her clit had her crying out, her whimpered pleas becoming more desperate when he pressed the head of his cock at her puckered opening.

She needed him to take her there. She needed to come. She needed relief from the razor-sharp pleasure that stole her ability to think.

Nothing mattered, except coming.

Shaking helplessly, she thrashed her head from side to side, but nothing allowed her to escape Blade's torment. "Please. Please." Her pleas for release grew increasingly ragged, chills racing up and down her spine and mingling with the heat at her slit as he pushed the head of his cock past the tight ring of muscle and into her.

Opening her eyes, she stared down at her dark and compelling lover, the man who excited her beyond belief. "Yes! More. Please. Hard, Blade. Hard."

Blade tossed the whip aside and ran his thumb over her clit as he slowly pressed his cock deeper. "I haven't heard an apology yet."

Crying out as he continued to press deeper, making her puckered opening sting and her ass burn all around him, Kelly threw her head back, the tingling at her slit and in her nipples driving her wild. "I'm sorry. Please. I'm so sorry. Please take me."

"I am taking you, love. After all, this is my ass to take, isn't it?"

"Yes. God, yes. Please!"

Blade's eyes narrowed, a half smile playing at his lips. "Please what? What do you want, Kelly? Spell it out."

Beyond embarrassment, and wanting nothing more than release, Kelly pressed her legs down against the leather and tried to rock her hips. "I want you to fuck my ass hard, damn it! You know what I need."

He withdrew slightly before slowly thrusting deeper. "That's right. I know what you need. I also know when to be forceful with you, and when to be gentle. I also know when you need this ass taken. It's mine, isn't it?"

"Yes. All yours." Tears pricked her eyes, the pressure building inside her until she thought she would burst. "Please let me come, Blade. Please. I'll do anything."

Blade smiled. "I know you will, love. Come for me."

Kelly screamed as he pressed deeper, her entire body stiffening as wave after wave of sensation washed over her.

Her ass clamped down on his cock, milking him as he fucked her ass with long, smooth strokes. "Yes. Yes. Yes."

So full. So hot.

He took her ass with a possessive arrogance that never failed to thrill her, his cock forging its way deep and forcing her ass to stretch to accept him.

It hit her with a force that left her breathless, the sharp tingling pleasure rippling through every inch of her body until even her fingers and toes tingled.

Perspiration covered her as she rode the waves, her orgasm holding her in its grip for what seemed like forever before releasing her in a rush of sensation.

His slow, steady thrusting continued, not letting her come down all the way, the brush of his thumb over her clit pushing her relentlessly back toward the edge again.

With her legs spread high and wide, she couldn't stop him, or even slow him down. Having no say in what he did, and trusting him implicitly allowed her to revel in every sensation.

He took her deeper. Harder. Faster.

Another brush of his thumb over her soaked clit sent her over again, forcing her to clamp down on his cock as her orgasm slammed into her.

Before she could completely come down, he moved his thumb faster, wrenching another orgasm from her.

"One more."

Shaking her head from side to side, she gripped the side of the table, too weak to even tighten her thighs again. "No more. No more."

"Yes. I want one more from you. You'll give it to me."

Blade ran his hands over her leather-covered thighs, making her wish she wore nothing at all. His eyes, so dark and intense, narrowed even more. "You'll give it to me, Kelly, because I command it."

He pinched her clit, sending sharp pleasure and pain through her, a sensation that thrilled her as much as it alarmed her. "I've been too lenient with you lately. You're going to have to get used to a firmer hand again—a hand that is going to give you a sound spanking for your defiance before the night is over."

Thrusting harder and deeper, Blade pulled back the hood of her clit and slid his fingers hard and fast over the swollen nub, the friction sending her over again in a rush of heat and sensation that tore a sob from her.

Trembling and weak, she whimpered through her orgasm, the sensations layering over each other becoming so intense that she knew nothing else.

She had no choice but to accept it, sucked into a world of erotic pleasure that pushed everything else aside.

She didn't know how much time had passed, but she gradually became aware of Blade's soft crooning voice close to her ear as he peeled her out of the tight leather. She blinked, surprised to find that he'd released her from the restraints without her knowing about it.

"That's my baby. I knew you could do it. Yes, love. I've got you. You're so beautiful, honey. No, baby. I've got it. Let me take care of you."

Before she knew it, he was lowering both of them into the large bathtub in the master bathroom, holding her close as he settled her on his lap.

Opening her eyes, she reached up to touch his jaw. "Oh, Blade. That was amazing. I love you so much."

Touching his lips to hers, he ran his hands over her breast and down to her belly. "I love you, too, Kelly, sometimes more than I can stand."

Lifting his head, he cupped her cheek, smiling faintly. "I adore you, love, and the thought of anything happening to you scares the hell out of me. I love our son, but I can't risk having any more. I need you too damned much."

Pressing a hand to her breast, he frowned. "Your breasts are full. You're going to be in pain if you don't feed Hawke tonight."

With a moan, Kelly arched into his slow massage. "I want tonight with you. I'll use the breast pump when I get out."

"I'll do it." Blade smiled at her look of surprise. "You belong to me, Kelly, and I'll take care of you. You scared me, baby, and it's not something I think I'm ever going to get over."

Warmed by the love shining in his eyes, Kelly cuddled close. "I'm fine, Blade. I promise. I love our son, too, but I have to admit, I'm kind of relieved that we won't be having any more children. I don't want to leave you a minute before I have to."

Blade bent her back over his arm, running his hands up and down her body. "I never thought I would love the way I love you. I never thought the need to possess would go so deep. I never thought the need to cherish would be so strong."

Cupping her cheek, he ran his thumb over her bottom lip, his hooded eyes glittering with emotion. "And every time I think I can't love you any more, I do. You've made me a better man, Kelly, a man who loves you with every fiber of his being."

Tears blurred her vision as he lowered his head, taking her lips in a kiss so sweet, it brought a lump to her throat.

Lifting his head, he smiled. "That doesn't mean I've forgotten about turning you over my knee tonight."

Recognizing the concern in his eyes at the tears in hers, and his attempt to lighten the atmosphere, Kelly nodded. Choking back a sob at the depth of her feelings for him, Kelly smiled through her tears. "I would be extremely disappointed if you did."

His love for her overwhelmed her at times, as did her love for him. "I'm so glad Jesse talked me into moving here."

Blade hugged her close. "So am I, love. So am I. I'll be forever grateful to her for bringing you into my life."

Kelly sighed, snuggling closer to her husband. Her lover. Her friend.

Life had changed for her so much since she met him.

He'd made her better, too. Stronger. Confident.

Secure in her husband's love, and in his arms, she closed her eyes and snuggled close again, smiling when his arms tightened around her.

There was no place she'd rather be.

THE END

WWW.LEAHBROOKE.NET

ABOUT THE AUTHOR

When Leah's not writing, she's spending time with family and friends, and plotting new stories.

For all titles by Leah Brooke, please visit
www.bookstrand.com/leah-brooke

For titles by Leah Brooke writing as
Lana Dare, please visit
http://www.bookstrand.com/lana-dare

Siren Publishing, Inc.
www.SirenPublishing.com

CPSIA information can be obtained at www.ICGtesting.com
Printed in the USA
BVOW04s1433080614

355763BV00005B/76/P

9 781627 413190